ALL THE GIRLS BEAU LOVED

ANGELICA ASHLEY

Table of Contents

PART THREE: MY I.NVISIBLE B.EST F.RIEND (THE PLAY THAT STARTED IT ALL)

This book is dedicated to
the girl waiting for a knock on her door
hoping it'd be him,
the woman learning to heal
from the fact it never was,
and
the ones that showed up on her doorstep
instead.

PART ONE:

JUST A BAND-AID

This book is a collection of three separate but interrelated stories, with an intriguing genre shift in the third part. They are to be taken as separate entities, dealing with similar themes through an ensemble of characters that are all connected through the title character Beau.

This book began as a simple one act play called My I.nvisible B.est F.riend that I wrote when I was 15. The play I wrote with the help of my best friend Persephone and got approved as the play we'd bring to drama competition during my senior year of high school. The play that now exists as Part Three of this book. The play that an audience never saw because the world went into lockdown two weeks before the planned opening night.

The rest of it came during a time of immense grief and healing. A need for an answer to the many questions that raced through my broken mind and heart that I knew would never be answered. This book is

the result of a mixture of coping and
imagination.

This book is a story about choices and how
decisions made by one person, intentionally
or not, can decide the fate of another.

This is All the Girls Beau Loved.

PART ONE, CHAPTER ONE

INT. CHURCH - DAY

YOUNG ADULT JAMIE, a 22-year-old woman, stands alone wearing a white dress in a hallway. She is looking over cue cards with shaking hands.

YOUNG ADULT JAMIE VOICEOVER: How did we get here? *(Pause.)* Did you know what you'd do?

Jamie goes to the nave of the church. She walks all the way to the front. Only when she gets to the front is the funeral revealed.

YOUNG ADULT JAMIE (V.O): *(tense)* Did you know this is where we'd be?

She walks to the casket.

YOUNG ADULT JAMIE (V.O): You broke your promise.

She leans over and looks in the casket.

EXT. SUBURBAN STREET - DAY

> *CHILD JAMIE, a 12-year-old realist,
> is leaning over and looking through
> her backpack. CHILD BEAU, a 12-year-
> old dreamer, is touching his knee
> looking hurt and he asks:*

CHILD BEAU: Do you think Ivy thinks scars are cool?

CHILD JAMIE: Maybe, but I doubt the scar you got cause you're too short for your bike, and you couldn't stop yourself from rolling down hospital hill, and ended up crashing, and scraping your knee is gonna be considered a "cool scar".

CHILD BEAU: Well, that's why I got it from saving a baby from a falling piano. Don't you remember? How I leapt and pushed the stroller out of the way and that's how I scraped my knee. True story.

CHILD JAMIE: *(concerned)* She's not dumb, is she?

CHILD BEAU: No, she's really smart actually. I'm the one who's dumb.

CHILD JAMIE: Why did you decide to try and bike down that hill? That was really stupid.

CHILD BEAU: *(embarrassed)* I overheard Ivy say she likes stunt guys the other day. So, I thought it'd make a good story to tell her.

Child Jamie facepalms.

CHILD BEAU: I kinda wish I broke a bone or something. Maybe get a cast, that would get her attention. Get her to sign it. Can't get her to sign a band aid, can I?

Child Jamie takes a bandage out and puts it on his knee.

CHILD BEAU: Ow, that hurts. What are you doing?

CHILD JAMIE: *(sarcastically)* Don't die now, it's just a band-aid.

CHILD BEAU: Can I just say, I almost died for real earlier? And what did my so-called best friend Miss Jamie Alison Wilson do? She laughed. What was that?

CHILD JAMIE: If you're so afraid of dying, let's make a deal, right now. Neither one of us can die, unless it's together and we're like super old.

CHILD BEAU: Like 40s old or like 90s old?

CHILD JAMIE: 90s old, idiot, we got too many things to do to only live till we're forty. Now, pinkie promise?

> *Child Jamie puts her hand up and Child Beau makes a pinkie promise.*

CHILD BEAU: *(in a very proper tone of voice)* I, Robert Beatrice Arden, pinkie promise to never die unless I'm an old person who has completed the game of life including all

the side quests with my best friend Miss
Jamie Alison Wilson.

*Beau gets up and on his bike. Jamie is
zipping up her bag and follows him by
getting on her bike. They start biking
around the neighbourhood.*

CHILD BEAU: But seriously, you hurt my knee
more with the band-aid. You put it on mean.

CHILD JAMIE: How could I have possibly put
it on "mean"?

CHILD BEAU: I bet Ivy knows how to put
band-aids on nicely.

CHILD JAMIE: It's just a band-aid, shut up,
Beatrice!

CHILD BEAU: It's a family name.

CHILD JAMIE: Well, stop getting injured and
I won't have to keep putting band-aids on
you.

They continue to bicker as they bike away towards the sunset.

EXT. BEAU'S BACKYARD - NIGHT
Child Beau and Child Jamie are lying next to each other on a picnic blanket. They are looking up at the moon in the night sky.

CHILD BEAU: Jam, do you think love is real?

CHILD JAMIE: I think so...

She looks at him with love in her eyes. He keeps staring at the sky and doesn't notice her.

CHILD BEAU: I think I'm in love with her.

CHILD JAMIE: Oh?

She turns to look at the sky instead of at him.

CHILD BEAU: Yeah, I mean, she's just so pretty and nice. I forgot my pencil case at home the other day and Ivy gave me one of

her pens. She didn't just let me borrow it;
she gave it to me. It's pink and sparkly. I
never use it because I don't want it to run
out. *(Beat.)* But I think loving someone and
being in love with someone might be
different.

He looks at her softly.

CHILD JAMIE: How so?

CHILD BEAU: I don't know the feeling feels
different when you love someone versus just
being in love with them. Like my mom used
to tell me that falling in love is
dangerous and will always end with pain
because when you fall down in any way, you
will get hurt.

CHILD JAMIE: Or you'll scrape your knee.

CHILD BEAU: Yeah, exactly.

CHILD JAMIE: Well, what did she say about
loving someone?

CHILD BEAU: She told me to find the person who is my "ocean".

CHILD JAMIE: Ocean, what does that mean?

CHILD BEAU: Like the person who calms you, that's constant, and beautiful, like how water always finds its way back to the ocean.

CHILD JAMIE: I love your mom.

CHILD BEAU: Me too.

Child Beau smiles softly.

CHILD JAMIE: Do you think you'll find your ocean?

CHILD BEAU: Mom said that you'll never know who it is until you do.

CHILD JAMIE: What?

CHILD BEAU: I don't know. That's just what she said.

CHILD JAMIE: Was your dad her ocean?

CHILD BEAU: *(thinking out loud)* I don't know. I think they were in love, for a long time, but I don't know if he loved her. She didn't talk about dad in that kind of way. Just that he gave her me. Told me about how he chased after her, they fell in love, he made mistakes, she took him back, and he didn't change.

I remember the blur of nights where she'd drive around town looking for him. I was too young to be left alone so I'd be asleep in the back. I'd get the bits and pieces of what happened all those nights. The driving, her crying, his slurred words. But every night when she'd put me back in bed, she'd kiss my head and tell me to forgive him. And then to forgive her for being so in love with him. I don't think I was meant to hear any of it.

And then when she got sick, dad started to go away for work. He comes back enough to not get me labelled as abandoned, but every

time he does, it's like I can hear her
crying in the background. And I hate him.

Child Beau takes a breath.

CHILD BEAU: *(painfully)* But I forgive him.
(Beat.) Because that's what she'd do.

*Child Beau wipes his tears away and
shakes his head.*

CHILD BEAU: I don't think he was her ocean.
I might not know much, but I know enough to
know it isn't about him. At least, I hope
it wasn't. I hope there was someone better.
Some perfect love that got away or
something. I think my mom deserved
something like that, you know. To have
experienced true real love at least once in
her life. I wish she just told me. That
might've been the point though. For me to
figure it out. I wish I knew her better.
For longer. I wish I could talk to her
again. She was the most magically beautiful
person who never made any sense. I mean,
everything she did was out of kindness and

love, and yet you never knew what she was
thinking or what she'd say.

CHILD JAMIE: *(with ease)* She always had the
best jokes too. My favourite one is the one
about the Italian chef.

CHILD BEAU: Oh yeah, did you hear about the
Italian chef who died?

BOTH: *(laughing)* He pasta way.

> *They laugh as they both turn to face
> each other. They hold hands and just
> lie quietly looking at each other.
> After a moment, Child Jamie says:*

CHILD JAMIE: I'm sorry your mom died.

CHILD BEAU: *(insecure)* Yeah, I'm sorry for
being so sad all the time. Thanks for still
being here and listening even if I'm a bit
repetitive.

CHILD JAMIE: *(reassuring)* I like listening to you talk, even the sad stuff. You can always talk to me, don't ever forget that.

CHILD BEAU: Do you think we'll be together forever?

CHILD JAMIE: Do you?

CHILD BEAU: I hope so. I hope I never lose you. You're nice.

CHILD JAMIE: You're nice too.

Child Beau and Child Jamie lie in the quiet for a moment. Child Jamie pulls away and sits up.

CHILD JAMIE: I better head home now.

CHILD BEAU: Okay, thanks for hanging out with me!

CHILD JAMIE: You don't gotta thank me.

CHILD BEAU: I know but still, thanks for being my best friend.

> *She smiles at him, but there's a sense of disappointment in her eyes.*

CHILD JAMIE: Yeah. Okay, good night, Beau. Don't stay up too late thinking about her.

CHILD BEAU: *(touch of pain)* Which "her"?

CHILD JAMIE: Just don't stay up too late. By the way, what we watching tomorrow night?

> *Child Beau walks her to the gate. He stands holding it open as their conversation continues.*

CHILD BEAU: 50 First Dates.

CHILD JAMIE: Again? That movie's weird.

CHILD BEAU: What? You love 50 First Dates! We watch it all the time.

CHILD JAMIE: No, you love it. That's why we watch it all the time. If it were me, we'd be watching Child's Play or something. But if I'm being honest, I think 50 First Dates is scarier.

CHILD BEAU: How is 50 First Dates scarier than Chucky?

CHILD JAMIE: Imagine waking up every day, on a boat, and you find out through a video that you're married to Adam Sandler.

CHILD BEAU: *(attempting to convince her)* But he's the man of her dreams and he makes her fall in love every day. It's romantic.

CHILD JAMIE: *(unimpressed)* It's Adam Sandler.

CHILD BEAU: *(lightly)* Go home already.

CHILD JAMIE: *(very playful)* I will. Bye. See ya. Go to bed and dream about Adam Sandler.

Beau rushes inside as Jamie gets on her bike and starts to bike home. Beau is sitting at the window at the front of his house and knocks on it. He gets Jamie's attention. She stops to look back at him and smiles. Beau smiles at her and waves until she starts biking away again. As Jamie bikes away, we hear:

JAMIE (PRE-LAP): Beau's mom used to say, God likes to pick the prettiest flowers for his garden, but she would also say that God gives the hardest battles to his strongest soldiers.

INT. CHURCH - DAY

Jamie stands at the front of the church and gives a eulogy.

YOUNG ADULT JAMIE: I'm not sure what He wanted for Beau. We all know he was very pretty, but not everyone knew about the other parts of him, except me, I guess. But no matter what, everyone who knew him will always remember his laugh, I know I will.

Whatever was happening, up or down, he always wanted to look towards the hopeful side. I never understood it fully, but I always admired his hopeless romanticism and the way he loved so deeply, like it was the only thing he knew how to do. Of course, there's no one he loves more than the love of his life, the girl he'll be loving forever even in death. One idea that's been keeping me sane through this process, is knowing that he's talking with his mom about her right now. Still I'm wishing I could listen to one of his rambles now. I guess from now on, he'll just have to listen to me, especially on those quiet nights, when the moon shines a little bit brighter.

Jamie starts to cry and turns to look away from the guests.

YOUNG ADULT JAMIE: Thank you for being here. Beau would've loved to see you all. I'll let someone else talk now.

*Jamie steps down from the altar and
sits down.*

YOUNG ADULT LILY: That was beautiful,
Jamie.

A small child's hand holds Jamie's.

EXT. ICE CREAM SHOP - DAY
*JAMIE, 18 years old, BEAU, 17 years
old, and LILY, 17 years old, Jamie and
Beau's only other friend, are eating
ice cream cones. Beau is texting and
is not fully present. Jamie's annoyed
and gets his attention by asking:*

JAMIE: *(to Beau)* You big idiot, why'd you
get such a big cone?

BEAU: *(in a baby voice)* Ice cream, very
yummy!

*Beau in the middle wraps his arms
around his two friends.*

LILY: Beau, stop it!

JAMIE: Ew, we told you; you're not allowed to talk like that ever!

BEAU: *(in his normal voice)* What, you don't like baby beau?

JAMIE & LILY: *(strongly)* NO.

   The girls push him away.

JAMIE: I don't like babies. I know for a fact I'm never having kids.

BEAU: *(baby voice)* That makes Baby Beau sad.

   Beau begins to mock a baby crying.

LILY: Nope, nope, I can't stand Baby Beau.

   Lily stands up.

LILY: *(to Jamie)* Oh, can I grab my wallet from your backpack?

JAMIE: Yeah, front big pocket.

Lily unzips the backpack. She pulls out a large bag of band-aids.

LILY: What's with the band-aids? Prepared much?

JAMIE: Oh, those are for Beau.

BEAU: *(with his mouth full)* I got funny blood.

JAMIE: Haemophilia, I think, is what it's called.

Beau nods his head like a little kid.

JAMIE: Basically, his blood can't clot for shit, so...

Jamie gestures to the bag. Lily puts it back.

LILY: Makes sense. You guys are weird. I'm happy we're friends. Anyway, I got a study sesh with my tutor, so I'll talk to you later, James. See ya, Beau.

Lily leaves.

BEAU: *(mocking Lily)* Talk to you later, James.

JAMIE: Oh, stop it, you're friends with her too.

BEAU: *(sarcastically)* No, she's smelly.

JAMIE: I like when she hangs out with us.

BEAU: Yeah, me too.

Beau wraps his arms around Jamie and makes smacking chewing sounds in her ear. They struggle holding their ice cream while tangling their arms around each other.

JAMIE: Stop, you're going to make a mess.

BEAU: So will you.

JAMIE: *(she loves him)* Ugh, I hate you!

IVY, an 18-year-old beautiful confident popular girl, walks by. Beau sees her and lets go of Jamie immediately. Jamie sits down looking uncomfortable as Beau walks toward Ivy.

BEAU: *(he's in love with her)* Hey Ivy!

IVY: Oh, hey kid, how are you?

BEAU: Good good, you know, I'm only like a year and a half younger than you.

IVY: Yeah, I know, I just think it's funny.

BEAU: Well, I just wanted to tell you that you did a great job last night. I could watch you sing over and over.

IVY: There are three more shows.

BEAU: And I will be at every one.

IVY: It's ten dollars a ticket.

BEAU: *(casually)* I got thirty bucks and
nothing better to do.

IVY: *(with a few giggles)* You are something
else, Beau.

BEAU: I'm serious. I'll be there.

IVY: Okay then, I'll look for you.

BEAU: *(cheeky)* Also, another thing. *(Beat.)*
Would you want to go to the dance with me?

IVY: *(bugging him)* With you?

BEAU: Yes, was that not clear?

    Beau smiles at her. Ivy smiles back.

IVY: Yeah, of course, I will.

    *Ivy kisses his cheek before walking
    away. Beau walks back to Jamie.*

BEAU: Is she gone?

JAMIE: Yeah, she's gone.

BEAU: Did you see that?

Beau does a goofy celebration dance and almost drops his ice cream again.

JAMIE: Oh my god, you're going to actually drop it, give!

He hands her the ice cream cone.

BEAU: Thanks, Jam!

JAMIE: No, thank you.

Jamie licks both ice cream cones and runs off. Beau runs after her.

INT. BEAU'S BEDROOM - NIGHT

Beau is picking his outfit for the dance and Jamie is lying on his bed watching him.

BEAU: *(stressed)* White or black socks?

JAMIE: Black, always black when it's formal. White socks are for basketball games.

BEAU: What do you know about basketball or formal events?

JAMIE: One, I was MVP in grade 9 and two, my mom drags me to all of her insurance scam social events.

BEAU: Is she really still doing that?

JAMIE: She really is.

BEAU: Didn't you only get that MVP because you were the oldest player on the girl's junior B team.

Jamie throws a pillow at him.

BEAU: Hey, I'm just bugging, I'll always trust you.

JAMIE: Will you trust me when I tell you I don't think you should go with Ivy?

BEAU: Jam, this has literally been the dream since Grade Seven.

JAMIE: I know, I just don't want you to be disappointed when it doesn't turn out the way you want it to.

BEAU: What are you trying to say?

JAMIE: Are you sure that Ivy is the girl you should be taking?

> *Jamie is playing with Beau's teddy bear and avoiding eye contact.*

BEAU: Of course, she's my dream girl. She's so smart, funny, and have you heard her sing, oh my god. This is my chance to make her fall for me. We're gonna dance all night. I'll be in my snazzy new outfit, and right at midnight, we're going to kiss under the mirrorball.

> *Jamie looks up at Beau. Beau is trying to tie his tie in front of a mirror.*

JAMIE: It's not going to be like that, this isn't one of your rom-coms.

BEAU: I'm not stupid, I know it won't be like in the movies. But, Jam, I get to go to the dance with Ivy. Ivy!

JAMIE: I know, that's why I'm worried.

Beau turns around to face Jamie.

BEAU: What's wrong with me going with Ivy?

JAMIE: It's Ivy. You're… you.

BEAU: Jam, why would you say that? That's so… You know what, it's getting late, you should go home.

JAMIE: Beau, oh come on, you know what I meant. You don't make sense together.

BEAU: *(vomiting words out)* We actually make a lot of sense together. We've been talking for the past few months. She thinks I'm interesting and funny. We like the same bands and shows. She doesn't think it's crazy to dream of being a writer. She makes me feel like I can do anything. When we talk, it just feels *(beat.)* perfect. I think she might be my actual soulmate.

JAMIE: You're making this up.

BEAU: You're just jealous because someone actually wants to go with me. I'm sorry that no one asked you to go but don't project your issues onto me, because I'm not you. I go to things and I talk to people. It can't always just be us hanging out forever.

JAMIE: You've been talking? Since when? Why didn't you tell me?

BEAU: After the last dance, I slipped up and told Ivy that I had a crush on her, well, I wasn't the one who told her, but she found out, and we swapped numbers and I didn't tell you, because I knew you'd just ruin it. So, I'm asking you to please go home. Please, Jam, just leave.

JAMIE: Wait, wasn't she still dating Austin then? *(Beat.)* Beau, was she still dating him when you started talking?

Beau doesn't answer.

JAMIE: You're an idiot. They broke up like a month ago.

BEAU: Ivy said they were basically not even together anymore because they hadn't hung out alone in months.

JAMIE: But were they broken up yet? Were you the reason they broke up?

BEAU: No, I wasn't the reason Austin broke up with her. I had nothing to do with it. And we didn't do anything wrong; we waited till after they were broken up.

JAMIE: *(stern voice)* What do you mean? Were you sending flirty texts? Were you emotionally and/or romantically invested in each other? Were you talking to each other about being soulmates? Were you doing any of this before Austin had broken up with her?

BEAU: Ivy didn't cheat. I would never let her do that. I wouldn't do that.

JAMIE: But you thought about it?

BEAU: I don't know, she would talk about being with me in the future and stuff, but that's not-

JAMIE: Why would she be talking to you like that? How could she even justify that?

BEAU: I'm her soulmate, Austin was just a high school sweetheart. But I'm her forever. She told me. And she did not ever cheat on him. She's not that kind of person. She waited till after they broke up to even kiss me.

JAMIE: Oh wow, sorry, she waited. That doesn't help her case, Beau. She doesn't care about you. She's just using you and then when she gets bored like she did with Austin, she'll do the same to you.

Beau can't look at Jamie right now.

JAMIE: Seriously, Beau. What were you even thinking?

BEAU: It's Ivy.

JAMIE: I know, you've been in love with her forever but really, is this what you want? To be her side piece-slash-rebound? You deserve better than that, Beau. Come on, like, really?

BEAU: Go home, Jamie. You don't know what you're talking about. You don't know Ivy like I know her.

Jamie gets up and starts getting ready to leave. Beau keeps struggling to tie his tie and Jamie is angrily shoving her stuff in her backpack.

JAMIE: *(sarcastically, then serious)* Fine, whatever, I hope it's the best night of your life and you get everything you ever dreamed of. Everyone knows her, everyone except you. How many times are you going to do this? How many soulmates could you possibly find in this life? I can't keep up with you. I can't keep picking you up off the floor after they break your heart, so don't go knocking on my door when she does. I don't even know who you are right now. You're not you. You're not Beau.

Jamie walks out and slams the door.

BEAU: Dammit, Jamie!

PART ONE, CHAPTER TWO

INT. SCHOOL GYM - NIGHT

Beau walks in with Ivy, who is wearing a dark blue dress. Jamie is sitting on the side wearing a beautiful sky-blue dress with Lily who is wearing pink. Beau waves at them. Jamie looks away. Beau brings his focus back onto Ivy.

BEAU: Jamie's here. Huh, she said she wasn't coming.

IVY: *(with judgement)* She looks cute.

BEAU: *(genuine)* Yeah, she does.

Beau glances over at Jamie and smiles. Beau catches himself smiling about Jamie and snaps himself out of it.

BEAU: Shall we dance?

IVY: Of course, kind sir.

Beau takes Ivy's hand, and they go onto the dance floor and start dancing. Beau tries to dance, but Ivy starts grinding against him. Beau gets very awkward and is trying his best to be respectful and keeps his hands off, but Ivy encourages him to touch her.

BEAU: So why did you start talking to me?

IVY: You're cute.

BEAU: Do you actually like me?

IVY: I'm dancing with you, aren't I?

Beau spins Ivy around to be face to face, holding her in place with his hands on her hips.

BEAU: No, seriously, Ives, do you really like me like that?

IVY: Yes, and to prove it, I'll let you know a secret.

BEAU: What?

IVY: *(whispering in his ear)* After the dance, we can hang out at my place. My mom's working tonight, so we can do anything. How does that sound?

> *Ivy kisses him. Jamie sees this and leaves the dance and hides in the bathroom. Jamie starts to cry in the mirror. She does her best to not ruin her makeup. Jamie returns to the gym and watches as Beau watches Ivy sing with the band. Lily finds her and grabs her hand and holds it.*

LILY: We can go. We don't have to stay, J.

JAMIE: We don't?

> *Jamie lets out a laugh as she tries not to cry again. As the girls walk toward the exit, Beau sees them. He contemplates going after them. He realises he must choose between Jamie and Ivy at this moment. He looks back and forth between the girls. He stands*

still watching Jamie and Lily walk out the door.

INT. IVY'S HOUSE - LATER THAT NIGHT

Ivy holds Beau's hand as they lead a group of Ivy's friends into the house. The group is chaotic and immediately makes themselves at home. They turn the music up loud and raid the fridge and cabinets. Ivy gets Beau to do a bunch of shots while she watches. They are having a good time before Ivy gets stolen away from Beau to dance by her friends.

IVY: Sorry!

BEAU: *(full of worry)* No worries.

Beau sits in the kitchen as more people rush in. He watches Ivy dance with her friends for a moment. She laughs loudly. Someone hands him a drink, he glances at the clock on the microwave, it is 11:00, he forces himself to drink whatever is in the

cup, he looks up again, it is 11:11.
He looks around at all the drunk and
high strangers in the room and feels
his heart begin to race before
sneaking outside.

EXT. IVY'S FRONT YARD- NIGHT

In a dizzy haze, Beau starts to walk
down the street. Ivy yells after him,
she is more sober than Beau.

IVY: Hey, kid! Where are you going?

BEAU: *(uncomfortable)* Sorry, it's just not really my scene. You know, all the party stuff, with the other stuff, I just… Just go have fun with your friends. I'm gonna go find some water and maybe apologise to Jamie. I was a real shitty friend the other day.

IVY: (cutting him off) Beau, do you wanna know the real truth about why I said yes to the dance with you, and why I like talking to you, and why I want to hang out with you tonight?

Beau stays silent.

IVY: I said yes because you're really nice.

BEAU: I'm nice.

IVY: Like really really nice. You're everything. I know tonight's the first night we've properly hung out, but it's you, just you. You are everything. Your smile. You always smile at me in the halls, and it just radiates off your face. Your entire face works together to create a masterpiece. Don't let me start on the way you dress with your cute sweaters and button up shirts, and your body, all of it is just an orchestra of "yes".

> *Ivy moves towards Beau and kisses him before continuing.*

IVY: Your lips, it's such a feeling of infinity to kiss them.

> *Ivy takes Beau's hands and leads him to sit down on the curb with her.*

IVY: Do I need to keep going or will you come back?

BEAU: I don't know about this, Ives.

IVY: Okay, well, your personality amazes me. You treat every situation as the best and you always manage to find the good in the bad. You have the ability to make anyone smile. You make me smile and you have given me something, no person has ever given me.

BEAU: And what's that?

IVY: Love at first sight.

BEAU: Really?

IVY: Maybe not like in the movies, but that's not realistic, I couldn't have actually fallen in love with you. I was in Grade Seven.

BEAU: So was I and I fell in love with you at first sight.

IVY: *(with disbelief)* No

BEAU: YES. I have been in love with you
ever since.

IVY: Well, fine, not love at first sight
then. You can have that. What you have
given me, in the time of us talking, is a
feeling of a future. A secure one, with a
house and backyard, the whole thing. The
feeling of wanting to spend my entire life
with you. The feeling of *absolute certainty*
that I would like to make you mine. That I
want you in every way and do everything.

Ivy kisses Beau again.

IVY: To be my firsts and your firsts for it
all.

And again.

IVY: To continue this life alongside you.
(Beat.) Through this entire experience of
talking to you, I have never once doubted

myself. Not even with the things that block
the things we both know we want.
And one more time.

IVY: But still so, if you wanna go, you can
go, I'll be waiting here like a brick wall
unwilling to break, no matter what.

BEAU: I think you better head inside to
make sure your house doesn't burn to the
ground.

IVY: Come with me then.

> *Ivy stands and starts to head inside.
> Beau takes a breath, looks up at the
> sky, it is a new moon tonight. There
> are only stars. Beau gets up and
> catches up with Ivy. A full view of
> the front of the house, we see the
> upstairs bedroom light turn on as the
> party continues downstairs.*

INT. JAMIE'S BEDROOM - THE SAME NIGHT
> *Jamie is lying on the floor of her
> room, still wearing her blue dress.*

Lily lies beside her. They each have one earphone in, and they are listening to Sick of Losing Soulmates by Dodie.

JAMIE: *(whispering)* Why did it have to be him?

LILY: Because it was *always* him.

Jamie curls herself up and lets the tears fall and finally ruin her makeup. Lily holds her as the sobs grow in violence.

INT. IVY'S FRIEND'S CAR - NIGHT

Music is blasting, Beau is sitting in the seat behind Ivy in the front passenger seat. LOU, Ivy's best guy friend, is doing doughnuts in a parking lot. Beau is anxiously gripping Ivy's hood.

IVY: Beau, stop, calm down, you're going to choke me out.

LOU: Ivy's a freak though, she probably likes it.

> *Lou has one hand on the steering wheel and puts his other hand around Ivy's neck playfully. Ivy laughs and lets him.*

IVY:(*to Lou*) Shut up. (*to Beau*) Kid, are you okay? Are you scared?

> *Beau doesn't answer.*

LOU: Well, I guess I should go faster. Beau clearly loves it. Ready, Ivy?

> *Lou and Ivy start wooing and the car goes faster. Beau is now having a panic attack, and his breathing has changed.*

BEAU:(*to Ivy*) Take me home. Please. Just take me home.

IVY:(*to Lou*) Okay, Lou, I think it's time to actually take him home.

LOU: Lame.

Lou starts driving away from the parking lot.

LOU: By the way, Beau, is it just BO or is it short for something?

BEAU: It's actually spelled BEAU, my mom liked it, but my name is actually Robert.

LOU: Robert, Bob, Rob, Robbie. I'll call you Robbie, it's cooler. Plus, how did you even get Beau from Robert?

BEAU: I would actually prefer it if you just called me Beau.

LOU: *(ignoring him)* So, Robbie, you're the one who stole Ivy from Austin?

Beau doesn't respond.

LOU: It's kinda funny, I thought it would've been me. But you beat me to it, Rob, good on you, kid.

*Ivy fixes her hair; Beau tries to grab
her hand to hold it. Ivy holds it for
a second and then drops it before
going back to dancing and singing to
the music playing. Ivy holds Lou's
hand. Lou and Ivy begin talking about
the party plans for next week. All the
music and conversation get replaced
with Beau's heartbeat. Beau is
exhausted, panicked, and is feeling
like he is in the wrong place.
Something is wrong here, but he can't
leave the moving car. He closes his
eyes and starts to take deep breaths.
He thinks of biking as the sun sets,
picnics in the park, and Jamie. Her
voice, her hugs, and her snort when
she laughs.*

EXT. JAMIE'S FRONT YARD - SUNSET
*Beau catches Jamie as she is putting
her garbage bin onto the street.*

BEAU: Jamie.

Jamie ignores him.

BEAU: Jamie, come on it's been months, please talk to me. I miss talking to you.

Jamie continues to ignore him.

BEAU: Come on, you're my best friend. You have to talk to me. We graduated and I didn't get to celebrate with you. Do you know how shitty that is? You just stop talking to me, like the eleven years of friendship meant nothing. (Pause.) So, I need us to talk now.

Jamie finally turns to Beau.

JAMIE: Do you really want me to talk, or do you want me to listen to you while you talk?

BEAU: I want you to talk.

JAMIE: Okay then. I'll talk. I think the craziest part about friendship is that you pick someone, and you just care about them. You get to know every single thing about them. The real shit you hide from your

other relationships. And you said it. I'm
your best friend, Beau. This friendship is
my deepest and most important connection. I
know nothing and no one else like I know
you. *(Pause.)* I know you... *I really know
you.* And yet I want you. More than I want
myself.

(hesitates, angry at herself)

You have been everything to me, for forever
and I don't know what else to do but tell
you even though I know I have no chance.
Our entire lives I've watched you watch
these girls and listen to you fall in love
with someone who wants nothing to do with
you over and over again. And I'm a huge
giant hypocrite because I've been doing the
exact same thing.

(anger builds into desperation)

I hate her because of you. And that's so
shitty. I hate that I hate her because
she's fine, she's a nice person, and I
don't really know her. But I know enough to
know that I hate that I hate her. And I
hate you. I hate you for never looking at
me the way you look at her. I hate you for
being this person. My person. My best

friend. Because if you were just some stupid boy, some fleeing crush I glanced at in an airport lobby, I wouldn't be here right now, asking you this. Can you please just love me the way I love you? Because I can't exist without you. I know it's so selfish. But I don't know what else to do.
(Beat.)
I love you, Beau. With every atom of my being, on every plane of existence, across every known and unknown universe, I love you. So, I'm asking, please, love me back.

> *Beau stands in a state of shock. Jamie is sobbing into Beau's chest. He holds her in a loose embrace. She looks up at him. He looks at her. The tension between them builds until Beau quietly reveals:*

BEAU: I- *(beat.)* Ivy's pregnant.

> *Jamie pushes Beau away.*

JAMIE: *(in disbelief)* What?

BEAU: *(happy, touch of pain)* It's mine…

JAMIE: *(painfully)* Beau…

BEAU: …and she's keeping it.

> *Silence fills the air; it stays silent
> for an uncomfortable amount of time.
> Beau and Jamie just stare at each
> other trying to decide what to say
> next. Jamie is tense with frustration
> and anger, while Beau is frozen with
> fear of losing his best friend. Beau
> believes this is a fixable situation,
> Jamie has lost every ounce of hope she
> had.*

JAMIE: *(tense)* When?

BEAU: What do you mean?

JAMIE: When did you get her pregnant?

BEAU: She just told me. She thinks it
might've happened the first time we...you

know. But we've been hanging out all summer
and I don't really keep track-

Jamie steps back from Beau.

JAMIE: When was that first? When she thinks
it happened?

BEAU: The night of the dance.

JAMIE: *(angry but not surprised)* Oh my god.
Really? Really.

BEAU: What do you want me to say? I'm being
honest here.

Jamie stands still and silent. Beau is
pacing.

BEAU: *(painfully)* Jamie, I missed you. I
thought of you every day and every night.
Every time, I saw the moon. Please say
something. I need you to help me out here.
Please.

JAMIE: *(tearfully)* You're going to be a great dad, Beau. But I can't do this.

BEAU: *(painfully)* Jamie, please. I need you.

Beau attempts to grab Jamie's arm but misses her and she continues to walk away.

JAMIE: I'll probably see you around still, but I can't do this. I'm so sorry. I can't be the person who cares about you right now.

Jamie walks away.

BEAU: *(desperate)* I was trying to end it when she told me. *(Beat.)* I'm so in love with her, but she-she's changed. She doesn't talk to me like she used to. I hadn't seen or heard from her for like two weeks before last night. I was done, I was so ready to leave, to give up and break up with her, but now I don't know what to do. Help me, Jam. Please just tell me what to do.

Jamie turns around again.

JAMIE: Beau, we both know what you'll do. You're you. It's a baby. It's your baby. And you love her. I know you, Beau, and I'll always care about you. If anything, you know how to find me. I'm sorry again, but goodbye, Beau.

> *Jamie walks away. Jamie stops at her door but does not turn around. Jamie goes inside. Beau walks away.*

PART ONE, CHAPTER THREE

INT. JAMIE'S BEDROOM - NIGHT

Jamie is crying in her room. Her parents come in and yell at her about her plans.

JAMIE'S MOM: Stop crying.

JAMIE'S DAD: I knew I never should have never let you talk to him. You said you were just friends. What did he do to you? Did he touch you? You know you're better than that, Jamie. You better be better than that.

JAMIE: *(fearfully moves away)* No, he didn't do anything to me. He never even thought about me like that. He literally told me that he's having a baby with Ivy.

JAMIE'S MOM: Why are you crying then? You're not the stupid one who got pregnant. You weren't cheated on. You weren't broken up with. You weren't even together. Why are you crying? Make it make sense.

JAMIE'S DAD: Your mother is right. You have no reason to cry, so stop it now, and focus. School starts in a month. Get a head start and forget about him. Don't be a stupid girl.

JAMIE'S MOM: If we catch you crying again, if you aren't focused, you'll be in trouble. We worked very hard to get you through high school, get you into a good university. All we ask for in return is your focus. Don't let some stupid boy ruin it. Stop crying now, you're being foolish, pray for forgiveness, and then go to sleep.

Jamie's mom leaves.

JAMIE'S DAD: We will see you in the morning. Good night, baby. We love you. We just want you to succeed. God bless you always. May the good God guide you. Jamie's dad kisses her on the forehead before leaving.

Jamie winces and then stops herself from crying and gets on her knees.

> *Jamie starts praying as her parents*
> *turn off her light and close the door.*

JAMIE: *(whispering through suppressed sobs)*
In the name of the father, the son, and the
holy spirit, please Jesus, take me away
from this pain. Please guide me to where I
need to be. Please take care of Beau for
me. I love him, please look after him.
Please take my feelings away. I want to be
a good daughter. I just want to be good.
Please make me good. I'll be good. I'll be
good for you, Jesus, please take me away
from here. Please.

INT. IVY'S BATHROOM - NIGHT

> *Ivy is looking at her stomach in the*
> *mirror. She has started to show. She*
> *doesn't know how to feel. Beau knocks*
> *on the door.*

BEAU: *(from the other side of the door)* You
okay in there, Ives?

IVY: *(not fine)* Yeah, I'm fine.

Ivy lowers her sweatshirt before leaving the bathroom.

INT. IVY'S BEDROOM - NIGHT

Ivy crawls back into bed. Beau joins her. Ivy pulls the blanket over her head.

BEAU: What is it?

IVY: I'm visibly pregnant.

BEAU: And?

IVY: People are going to know.

BEAU: *(trying to be funny)* They were going to find out eventually, you know, when the baby starts to fall out of you.

IVY: *(from under the blanket)* You're the worst.

BEAU: I'm sorry. I was trying to…

IVY: IT'S NOT FUNNY. GO AWAY. I'M TIRED OF YOUR STUPID JOKES TRYING TO MAKE ME FEEL BETTER ALL THE TIME. IT'S NOT WORKING. GET. OUT.

BEAU: I'm really sorry. I'll go. Just let me know if you need anything.

> *Ivy is silent. Beau kisses her head and then leaves her alone. There is a sound of clatter from the kitchen. Ivy removes the blanket off her head and wraps it around herself. She walks downstairs. Beau is picking up pots and pans from the floor. Ivy laughs.*

BEAU: Hello. I was going to bake you a cake to show my appreciation. But the cabinets threw up.

> *Ivy turns around. Beau puts the rest of the stuff away. Ivy goes and starts playing Our House by Crosby, Stills, Nash & Young on her phone. She wraps the blanket around him, and they dance in the kitchen.*

IVY: You know, it's a nice life. I see it all. You and me, and the baby.

> *Ivy sings along with the song. Beau holds Ivy tightly and gets tears in his eyes.*

IVY: Don't bake a cake *(beat.)* and stop crying, it's not very manly.

> *Beau wipes his tears.*

BEAU: I wasn't. I promise.

INT. CHURCH - DAY

> *Jamie is in the bathroom talking on the phone, struggling to hide her emotional state.*

YOUNG ADULT JAMIE: Hello, yes, this is Jamie. It is an honour to work on this project with you, sir. Thank you for the opportunity. Yes, yes, I am looking forward to the rest of it, sir. Thank you for being so understanding of the situation. I really appreciate it, sir.

YOUNG ADULT JAMIE: I would actually like to talk to you soon about a possible candidate for the trial. *(Beat.)* Yes, thank you, talk to you soon, thank you again, sir. *(Beat.)* Bye now.

Jamie lets herself cry after hanging up the phone. Before cleaning herself up and walking back out to the rest of the funeral.

INT. IVY'S BEDROOM - NIGHT

Beau is sleeping. Ivy is sitting up against the wall on their bed. She is rubbing her belly and singing Sweet Caroline quietly. Beau wakes up.

BEAU: Hey, why are you still awake?

IVY: My mind's too quiet.

BEAU: Isn't that a good thing?

IVY: *(vulnerable)* It's unsettling, it's just quiet. I don't like it. I can't sleep. Growing up, there was always either a party going on or a fight or someone laughing because they were high. But when it was quiet, it meant they left me alone in the house. When there was noise, I knew I wasn't. Mom didn't really like to party, dad did, and so the house got really quiet after he left. And it's just a different type of discomfort, to listen to the quiet and know how unhappy she was. I've never made her happy. My sister made her happy. But my sister went away and then she never called us back. She left exactly like dad did. Then it was just mom and me.
(frustration builds as she speaks)
I'd listen to my mom's cries every night, except for the times, she'd drink, and the crying would stop, and I knew it was my cue. My cue to go downstairs and clean up the house, put the bottles in the recycling, do the dishes, wipe off her makeup, make sure she's on her side so she doesn't choke on her own vomit, and throw a blanket over her passed out body. And then

finally get the three hours of sleep before
going to school.

My sister used to warn me about mom, tell
me that mom was the crazy one, that mom
drove dad away. But I think dad was scared.
Scared that mom would leave him, so he left
first. He ran before she could kick him
out. And my sister followed him. But I
stayed. *(Pause.)* I did. I stayed.
I'm sorry. She's sober now, thank God,
but... still. The quiet doesn't help.

> *Ivy wipes the tears from her eyes
> before she lies down to be face to
> face with Beau and looks deeply in his
> eyes.*

IVY: I think I might love you, Beau.

BEAU: I love you too.

> *Beau and Ivy kiss.*

BEAU: Do you wanna keep talking? Or watch a movie? We could put something on so it's not so quiet.

IVY: No, you go back to sleep, you got work in like four hours, I'll be fine.

BEAU: Nah, I'll stay awake with you. I'll just call in.

IVY: Okay.

Beau caresses Ivy's cheek and kisses her forehead.

IVY: Do you think I'll be a good mom?

BEAU: I mean, as a kid whose mom died, and dad is barely here. If you stay, that's like 75% of it so yeah.

Beau yawns, closes his eyes, and is falling asleep as he says:

BEAU: You'll be good.

IVY: Can we name her Caroline?

BEAU: We can name her whatever, just promise that it'll be me, you, and her, forever. Can you do that?

> *Beau falls asleep before Ivy gives an answer. Ivy looks at Beau and rubs her belly with concern and anxiety. Ivy closes her eyes to try to sleep.*

INT. IVY'S HOSPITAL ROOM - NIGHT

> *Beau walks in. Ivy is lying in bed, clearly upset. The baby is lying in a hospital bassinet.*

BEAU: Hey, Ives.

> *Ivy stays quiet and does not look at Beau. Beau tries to put his hand on Ivy's back. Ivy moves away from him. Beau goes to meet his baby in the bassinet.*

BEAU: (*sweetly and softly*) Hello.

Beau reads the name tag on the bassinet. A bit confused but goes with it. Beau washes his hands before picking up his newborn baby. As Beau picks up the baby, there is a sense of calm, there is no nervousness or fear in Beau. Beau and his baby are perfect.

BEAU: Hello, baby girl. I guess mommy hasn't named you yet. That's okay. I'm sorry, I'm late to show up. Mommy didn't let me know when you were coming, and daddy was at work. But I'm here now.

NURSE walks in.

NURSE: Are you the dad?

Beau turns around to face the nurse.

BEAU: Yes, yes I am.

NURSE: Okay, perfect. Now that you're here, is it time to give this beautiful baby a name?

Ivy does not move.

BEAU: Yeah, just give us one second.

Nurse takes the baby from Beau and puts the baby back in the bassinet. Beau goes and kneels beside Ivy's bed to look at her face to face.

BEAU: *(softly)* Hey, Ives. Are you ready to name our baby?

IVY: *(numb)* I don't care.

Ivy does not move. Beau tries to hold her hand. She pulls her hand away.

BEAU: Okay, last week, we chose one. Is that one okay? Is that one good?

IVY: *(still numb)* I said, I don't care.

BEAU: *(kindly)* Well, we can wait if we need to.

IVY: *(sharply)* No, name her. I don't care.

BEAU: *(calmly)* Okay, I'll name her.

Beau kisses Ivy's forehead before standing up and going to the nurse with the papers.

NURSE: Okay, last name?

BEAU: Ellis, hyphen, Arden

Ivy sits up in bed.

IVY: Just Arden.

BEAU: What? You don't want her to have your last name?

IVY: No. And do not fight me on it.

BEAU: I thought you didn't care.

IVY: I don't want the baby to have my last name. I want it to have yours. End of discussion.

Ivy lies back down.

BEAU: Okay then, so her last name will be
Arden. And her first name will be Caroline.

NURSE: Any middle names?

   Beau looks at Ivy.

BEAU: Jamie.

   Ivy still has not moved.

INT. IVY'S BEDROOM - NIGHT
   *Ivy is lying in her bed watching old
   videos of her singing. Beau comes home
   still in his work uniform and cuddles
   her.*

BEAU: Hey, Ives. What ya watching?

IVY: Some old videos of me singing.
BEAU: Oh?

IVY: I was a singer. I was supposed to go
to New York or LA or Paris or anywhere.

BEAU: You could still do it.

IVY: What do you mean, I could still do it?

BEAU: You could still sing, post videos, or find a place to sing. The city's big enough here, I bet there's somewhere to go.

IVY: No one's gonna wanna hear me sing.

BEAU: Ives, every time you stepped on that stage in high school, every single person in the room didn't blink or breathe.

IVY: Thanks for saying that.

BEAU: I mean it too.

IVY: I know you do.

BEAU: Oh, and I made you something.

IVY: For why?

BEAU: One year of us being official.

IVY: Oh no, I didn't realise.

BEAU: That's okay, we have a weird timeline
so it's okay that you didn't. But yeah,
it's been a year since we started hanging
out. So, here.

*Beau hands her a necklace. It is a
penny on a pop can tab with a black
string. It has an image of a flying
bird on it. Beau puts it on her. From
now on, Ivy will always be wearing it.*

BEAU: I know it's not much. I promise
someday I'll get you something proper.

IVY: No, this is perfect. My new lucky
charm.

Ivy smiles and Beau kisses her cheek.

PART ONE, CHAPTER FOUR

INT. IVY'S LIVING ROOM - NIGHT

Ivy walks in. She is wearing a red dress. Beau is folding laundry at the dining table.

BEAU: How did it go?

Ivy smiles.

IVY: I got it.

Ivy and Beau jump up.

BEAU: You got it.

IVY: I got it. I'm a singer at a real lounge.

BEAU: Woo, my girl's a lounge singer. She's a singer.

Beau kisses her. Ivy smiles slightly.

IVY: One thing though, is that it isn't guaranteed that I'll get paid doing this. It's basically just tips.

BEAU: That's okay, I can get another job.

IVY: Are you sure, Beau?

BEAU: You are the mother of my child, if I can help you achieve your dreams in any way, you can trust in me. For you, I'd do anything. You have no idea.

IVY: So, it will be okay. And I can be a singer?

BEAU: Yes.

>   *Ivy celebrates.*

INT. BAR - NIGHT

>   *Beau is sitting at the bar watching Ivy sing. Beau's dad sits down next to him. Beau looks over and says:*

BEAU: How are you already drunk? Didn't you just get here?

BEAU'S DAD: You can start drinking anytime and anywhere, my friend. Here.

*Beau's dad hands him an envelope
filled with 5 000 dollars cash. Beau
looks confused.*

BEAU: Why?

BEAU'S DAD: I know you hate me.

BEAU: I don't hate you.

BEAU'S DAD: Don't lie. Your mother hates liars. I'm a shit dad. Might as well accept it and move on. You got a kid now, and her mom's a singer for Christ's sake and you're... you. So, I'll help you out. I'll hand over any extra cash I got.

BEAU: I'm not taking your money.

Beau hands the money back.

BEAU'S DAD: Get rid of that pride of yours. Take the money, my grandkid deserves better, let me do that. I got money to give. Take it. Burn it for all I care, just take it away from me and then I'll leave.

Beau hesitates but takes the money.

BEAU: Where'd you get this? You got a good gig lately, or what?

BEAU'S DAD: It's from your mom.

Beau looks confused and saddened.

BEAU: Mom?

Beau's dad orders a beer.

BEAU'S DAD: She was saving up for you to go to school, but I thought with the kid, it was time to just give up and give you the money. Just don't let that girl on stage waste it away.

BEAU: What's your problem with Ivy?

BEAU'S DAD: It takes one to know one, kid. And I know she's something like me. Just promise me something.

BEAU: What?

BEAU'S DAD: Promise me, don't be your mom. She gave me too many years.

Beau's Dad takes a sip.

BEAU'S DAD: I'm not stupid, I see how you look at me. No matter what I do, I'm that drunk in the front seat making your mom cry. I see him too. *(Beat.)* Just don't let Ava or whatever-

BEAU: It's Ivy.

BEAU'S DAD: Don't let Ivy take too much from you. You are the carbon copy of your mother. Love her, but don't ever let her consume you. She will never forgive herself. And you will never forgive her.

Beau's dad gets up and leaves. He leaves his beer behind. Beau puts the money in his bag and turns back to watch Ivy sing. Ivy is singing Love of my Life by Queen. Beau smiles at her and Ivy stares at the spotlight and does not look at Beau. Beau takes a sip from his dad's leftover beer.

INT. JAMIE'S BEDROOM - DAY

Jamie, with headphones on, is moving out of her parents' house. We watch her sort her belongings into take or leave piles. Leaving things like her trophies and proof of accomplishments, things her parents gave her, and clothes she no longer fits, and only taking a suitcase of clothes and a few small boxes of trinkets. At the back of her closet, she finds a box filled with mementos from her friendship with Beau. She sits on the floor and looks through the items. She reads a page from her diary.

JAMIE (V.O): Dear Diary, Today, Beau and I went thrift shopping and bought each other outfits. I dressed him up like a nerd, cuz that's what he is. LOL. He chose a big wedding dress for me. And then when we were eating lunch in our outfits, he said that his mom was the most beautiful person in

the whole universe. He said I looked like
her. He got kinda sad after he said that. I
think he misses her; she died last year. I
don't know how this works, but Jesus if you
read my diary, please give Beau's mom a hug
and tell her that her son misses her. Also
thank her for making her son such a cute
boy. Actually, don't tell her that. Okay, I
gotta go to sleep now, Beau and I are going
camping tomorrow and we're leaving early.
So good night, diary. Thanks.
With love and honesty, Jamie.

*She picks up her phone and types out a
text to reach out to Beau.*

JAMIE (TEXT): Happy birthday, I hope you're
doing well. I miss you.

She erases it and then types again.

JAMIE (TEXT): Hey, I'm sorry. Hope you're
having a good birthday. I miss you.

She erases it and types again.

JAMIE (TEXT): Happy birthday. I miss you. I love you.

She pauses and reads it over and over before erasing it. She opens her laptop and starts typing.

JAMIE (V.O): Dear Journal, I miss him. But I don't know if I should. I regret leaving him when he needed me, but I still think it was the right thing for me to do. I needed to go, but I won't lie, every day, I wish he'd call or show up. I miss talking to him. I miss my best friend. I miss him. With love and honesty, Jamie Alison Wilson.

Jamie sits and stares at what she's written. She gets up and packs up the mementos. She pushes the box to the keep pile. Jamie's mom comes in.

JAMIE'S MOM: You know, you don't have to move out yet.

JAMIE: I know, but I want to.

JAMIE'S MOM: But you could take the classes online, you could stay. We're going to miss you. Your dad is getting sick again. Having you home would be a great help. If you do classes online, you could get a job and help us with the bills.

JAMIE: I am not staying, mom. *(Beat.)* You used to ask every day, what my plan was, where I was going, if I found a place yet, and now what, because you need the help, you're asking me to stay. You're not going to miss me. You're going to miss having the spare change and parts. I am going and I'm sorry, but *(pause.)* I don't think I'll be coming back.

JAMIE'S MOM: Good. *(Pause.)* If you can't find reason to care for your own parents, then you are not the girl I raised. I have done nothing but care for you, protect you, and teach you. I have provided everything you have ever needed. Ungrateful child.

Jamie's mom leaves. Jamie picks up the box of mementos and takes it to the car first.

INT. IVY'S BEDROOM - NIGHT

Beau comes home and Ivy is sitting on bed on her laptop looking at plane tickets. She closes her laptop when Beau sits down.

BOTH: Hey.

Beau sits next to her, and Ivy kisses him. Ivy begins to apologise by saying:

IVY: Look, I'm so sorry about last night. I hope you can forgive me, my love. That wasn't me. You know that I love you, right? I am the luckiest girl in the world to be loved by you. You are my pride and joy. I would never want to intentionally hurt you.

BEAU: Ives, you left me alone again. You promised we'd have the night, just you and

me. And what was it? Who was it? Who was
more important than my 18th birthday?

IVY: I am going to change, for you, Beau.
I'll stop going out and I'll never hurt you
ever again. It hurt me so much to hurt you.
And I hate myself for everything I've put
you through. I understand if you hate me
too. But please don't. Please don't hate me
because I love you and I don't know what
I'd do. I promise I'll be better.

Ivy kisses Beau.

BEAU: I love you too, I forgive you, and I
will never leave you. But I'm so tired of
waiting for you. I'm tired of getting my
hopes up. Don't make any more promises you
can't keep. I love you so much, but I don't
know how long I can keep doing this if
things don't change. I feel like you don't
even love me, I'm just here. Like nothing I
do will ever be enough.

Ivy grabs a box from her bag.

BEAU: What's this?

IVY: I saw it in a shop window the other day and I had to get it for you.

> *Beau opens the box and takes out a small vintage glass music box. He opens it and it plays Love of My Life by Queen.*

BEAU: I love it.

IVY: I love you.

> *Beau and Ivy lay down and cuddle.*

IVY: I like when you wear these pants, you look good in them.

BEAU: You said that when I bought them, remember?

IVY: Oh yeah? Are you sure it was me?

BEAU: Why do you think I wear them all the time?

IVY: You don't have to do that, you know.

BEAU: What?

IVY: Do things for me, I'm not…

BEAU: Not what?

IVY: Nothing, never mind.

> *Beau yawns and closes his eyes then falls asleep. Ivy stays put in his arms and checks if he's actually asleep. Ivy gets out of bed to check on the baby sleeping in the corner of the room. Ivy stares at her small baby before looking back at Beau asleep in bed:*

IVY: *(under her breath)* I'm not yours.

INT. JAMIE'S HOUSE - DAY
> *Jamie and Lily are looking at a house for rent. It is a one-bedroom house.*

LILY: We have to be at the wrong house. There's no way that this place is $850 a month.

JAMIE: With heat and water included.

LILY: Oh, I hope you get it. It's so you.

JAMIE: What. Cheap?

LILY: No, it's cute.

> *Jamie and Lily continue looking around.*

LILY: Ooo, this could be your office, instead of that sad corner in your apartment. I'm so excited for you.

JAMIE: I might not get it, Lil. I'm just applying for it.

LILY: Nah, you'll get it.

> *Jamie stands in the bathroom and smiles at herself in the mirror.*

JAMIE: I hope so. This is a nice bathroom.

INT. IVY'S BEDROOM - NIGHT

Beau is soothing baby Caroline as she screams. Beau is gentle and patient. Ivy walks in dressed up with her hair and makeup done.

BEAU: Where are you going? You don't have any gigs tonight.

IVY: Out.

BEAU: Again? With who?

IVY: Friends.

BEAU: When will you be back?

IVY: Late.

BEAU: Can I get more than just one-word answers?

IVY: No.

BEAU: You're never home, Ives. I know we compromised, but I thought on the nights you weren't singing, you'd be here. I always take care of her, and when I'm at work, your mom takes her. What about you?

IVY: The baby's fine. You have her and if you don't, my mom does. You said it yourself.

BEAU: You ever think maybe we'd like the night off? We took on a lot so you could do this. I gave up going to school this year so I could get more hours at work to support you and Caroline. Is it really too much to ask to see you more than when you're asleep or getting dressed or coming home drunk? I know this is important, but please, give us some time with you.

> *Ivy and Beau argue and talk*
> *simultaneously.*

IVY: I've invited you to join before-

BEAU: So, Caroline loses-

IVY: -but you're the one who refuses.

BEAU: -both of us every night-

IVY: You shut me down when I try-

BEAU: -to parties-

IVY: to make you part of my life.

BEAU: -and alcohol-

IVY: I want you to hang out-

BEAU: -and drugs.

IVY: -with my friends-

BEAU: I'm not interested-

IVY: -and see how happy-

BEAU: -in meeting anyone-

IVY: -I am out there.

BEAU: -whose hobbies-

IVY: But no, I'm the bad guy-

BEAU: -include making bad decisions that affect-

IVY: -for choosing myself and-

BEAU: -my family.

IVY: -my happiness.

BEAU: It breaks my heart-

IVY: How many times are we going have-

BEAU: -that you don't find-

IVY: -this fight. I've told you-

BEAU: -happiness here with me-

IVY: -over and over. I need to go out-

BEAU: -and her.

IVY: -and just feel like myself and my own person, when I'm here, who am I?

> *Beau begins to cry and beg. Ivy is angry and yelling.*

BEAU: You're a mom.

IVY: No, who am I?

BEAU: Her mom.

IVY: Who am I?

BEAU: She needs her mom.

IVY: Who am I?

BEAU: She needs you. Just hold her for a second.

IVY: Who am I, Beau?

BEAU: You've gone out every night this week. And last week, -

IVY: I don't know-

BEAU: -you didn't come home-

IVY: -who I am here.

BEAU: -for 3 days.

IVY: Answer the question!

BEAU: And the week before that when you did
come home, -

IVY: Who am I?

BEAU: -you came home drunk. You were here,
-

IVY: You aren't listening.

BEAU: -but you weren't here. Be here.

IVY: Listen, who am I?

BEAU: Just stay tonight. Please. Please.
Just stay with me.

IVY: I have to go.

BEAU: I love you, don't leave us again.

*Ivy slams the door as she leaves. The
baby starts crying again. Beau calms
the baby.*

BEAU: (tearfully) Shh, it's okay, dad's
here. I love you and I know mama loves you
too. She's just not doing good right now.
But she'll come back. She'll figure it out.
And she'll love you when she spends some
time with you. She will love you.

*Beau dances around with the baby. The
baby keeps screaming. Ivy's mom knocks
on the door then comes in shaking a
baby bottle.*

IVY'S MOM: I made a bottle. Do you want me to take her so you can take a break?

BEAU: No, it's okay, I got her. Thanks though.

> *Ivy's mom pats Beau on the back and kisses Caroline's forehead before leaving the room. Beau sings Caroline's Lullaby.*

BEAU: Just stay with me/And I'll hold you tight/Just stay with me/While the stars dance outside/Hold my hand in yours/Promise to hold on/Close those pretty eyes/Sleep, my Caroline/Just stay with me/And I'll hold you tight/Just stay with me/While the stars dance outside

INT. JAMIE'S HOUSE - NIGHT

> *Lily walks around the very bare house and peeks into the empty office.*

LILY: You still haven't bought that big desk?

JAMIE: Yeah, I don't know. I wanted the comfy couch more.

LILY: It is very comfy. Good decision making.

Jamie and Lily sit on the couch with a gap in between them. Lily notices and asks:

LILY: Do you still miss him?

JAMIE: Yeah, why?

LILY: You left a Beau shaped space between us.

JAMIE: Yeah, I guess I did. Sorry.

LILY: That's okay. *(Beat.)* Sometimes I miss him too. Probably not as much as you. It's more that I miss you.

JAMIE: What do you mean you miss me? I'm still here.

LILY: But you're different without him.
Nothing crazy, just like there's something
a bit off. Like when you eat a sandwich,
but you forgot to put the mayo on it, and
so you bite into it and you're like "yum,
very good sandwich, but oh no, where the
mayo?"

JAMIE: Yeah, I know what you mean.
Sometimes I do feel like a sandwich. An
idiot sandwich.

LILY: I don't think you're an idiot
sandwich. You're a sad sandwich who made a
tough decision but is still allowed to feel
sad. You are a valid sad sandwich. But the
question is would you let him back in if he
did come back into your life?

JAMIE: I think the real question is "Is he
ever going to come back?"

EXT. THE PARK - DAY

> *Ivy's mom is sitting on a bench
> watching Beau and Ivy play with*

*Caroline on the baby swing. Ivy comes
and sits next to her.*

IVY'S MOM: He's a good one. You guys look
so happy.

IVY: It's weird to think that in a week,
I'm leaving him. *(Pause.)* I bought the
plane tickets, mom.

*Ivy puts her head on her mom's
shoulder. Ivy's mom sits there
quietly.*

IVY: It's a very nice life.

*Ivy and her mom sit together for a
moment watching Beau and Caroline.*

IVY: But it's not mine.

*Ivy returns to Beau and Caroline. Ivy
and Beau laugh together while they
play with Caroline. Beau kisses Ivy's
cheek and looks at her with eyes full
of love.*

PART ONE, CHAPTER FIVE

EXT. IVY'S HOUSE - DAY

Beau comes home. All his belongings are out on the driveway. Beau runs to the door and starts frantically knocking.

BEAU: *(confused and frustrated)* Ivy! Why is my stuff out here?

Ivy's mom opens the door with Caroline in her arms. She hands Caroline to Beau.

IVY'S MOM: Beau, I'm sorry. She left. You have to go now.

BEAU: *(in denial)* Oh, come on, she'll be back tonight. If not tonight, tomorrow, or next week. She does this all the time. You know her, just help me move this stuff back in.

IVY'S MOM: *(heartbroken)* Not this time, she's gone, properly this time. She's not coming back.

BEAU: Where did she go?

IVY'S MOM: You know I can't tell you that.

BEAU: She just left?

IVY'S MOM: She's been planning this for a while. If it's worth anything, I tried to talk her out of it. But she just… I'm sorry. Just promise me that you'll take care of my granddaughter. You're a good man; my daughter just isn't a good woman.

> *Ivy's mom hugs Beau. Beau starts crying.*

BEAU: I'm sorry.

IVY'S MOM: *(crying)* You're okay. I'm so sorry too. I'm really so sorry. I wish it was different. I wish it was all different. But it's this. It's always this. I've already said my goodbye to Caroline, but I can help you pack your car.

BEAU: Why'd you say goodbye? You're her grandma and I would never keep her from you. Once we're settled somewhere, I don't know yet, but you can visit us anytime.

IVY'S MOM: *(heartbroken, trying to stay strong)* No, I can't. There's no good explanation, but this is going to have to be goodbye forever, Beau.

> *Beau puts Caroline in her car seat in the car. Beau and Ivy's mom start packing Beau's stuff into the car, there isn't much. Ivy's mom goes to talk to Caroline.*

IVY'S MOM: *(to Caroline)* I'll love you forever, baby girl. I hope even if we never meet again, you will always know that you are loved. I love you. And be more like your dad, not your mom, okay? Be kind to your dad.

> *Ivy's mom buckles Caroline into her car seat. Beau picks up his cell phone*

and tries to call his dad. A woman's voice picks up and says:

WOMAN ON THE PHONE: Hello?

BEAU: Hi, it's Beau. Is my dad home?

WOMAN ON THE PHONE: I'm sorry, who is this?

BEAU: Beau Arden, my dad is Robert Arden.

WOMAN ON THE PHONE: No, I'm sorry, wrong number.

The woman hangs up the phone. Beau hugs Ivy's mom.

BEAU: I'm sorry again. Thank you for taking us in. Thank you for all the help. We really appreciated it. We love you. We'll miss you. Please take care of yourself.

IVY'S MOM: Don't worry about me, Beau. I'll be okay, I'll always be okay. You be good. Don't ever change, my sweet boy.

Ivy's mom goes to stand at the porch as she
starts to cry. Beau kisses Caroline's
forehead before getting in the driver's
seat. He makes another call.

BEAU: Hey, it's Beau.

INT. JAMIE'S LIVING ROOM - NIGHT
*Jamie is asleep on her couch with a
psychology textbook in her hand. There
is a loud knock on her door. Jamie
answers the door to see Beau with a
baby carrier in hand.*

BEAU: Hi, Jamie. I'm sorry to show up like
this.

*Jamie stands still trying to process
who's in front of her.*

BEAU: *(desperate)* Ivy left. I know we
haven't talked in a year. I should've
called, but she just left, and I don't
know, I know you hate me, and this was a
dumb idea. I just didn't know what to do.
My dad apparently changed his number, so I

messaged Lily and thank God she gave your real address, and I've been meaning to reach out to you, but everything was happening, and my entire life was about the baby and Ivy and then *(beat.)* she left us.

Jamie hugs Beau.

JAMIE: *(reassuring)* I don't hate you.

BEAU: *(happily surprised, but still unsure)* Really?

They end the hug slowly.

JAMIE: *(comfortably)* Just get inside, we can unpack everything you just said later, but right now, you and your baby look cold.

BEAU: My daughter.

JAMIE: You have a daughter.

BEAU: I forgot you haven't met yet. *(Beat.)* This is Caroline Jamie Arden.

JAMIE: Her middle name is Jamie?

BEAU: Yeah, it is. I missed you. I thought about you every day. Every time Caroline did anything, I just wanted to call you and tell you about it. I'm sorry, my life had to go to shit before I showed up. I really didn't mean to dump any of this BS on you. I didn't know where to go.

Beau looks at Jamie for a moment.

BEAU: Jamie, I wish that I wasn't stupid. You're the one person in my life that ever made sense. I'm sorry, Jamie, you're my-

JAMIE: *(interrupting Beau)* Don't. Don't say it. Just let it be unsaid. You're back, that's all that matters right now. Save the dramatic speeches for later.

BEAU: *(about to cry)* I know it won't be the same. But I'm glad it's something again.

JAMIE: Me too, Beau

BEAU: *(crying)* Can I get another hug?

JAMIE: Of course, you can.

> *Beau hugs Jamie and keeps holding her as he lets his tears fall. Jamie holds him tighter as he falls into her.*

BEAU: *(softly)* Can we stay with you? Even just for tonight.

JAMIE: Yeah. Yeah, you can. For as long as you need. Promise me that we will never apart for that long again. I don't think the universe will take it.

> *Beau lets go of Jamie, backs up, and wipes his tears. They make a pinkie promise.*

BEAU: *(relieved)* Thank you.

JAMIE: No, thank you.

> *Jamie looks at Caroline in her car seat.*

BEAU: Do you want to hold her?

JAMIE: Yes, can I?

Jamie picks up Caroline.

JAMIE: *(softly, to Caroline)* Hello, baby girl. It is very nice to meet you.

BEAU: *(excited)* She likes you.

JAMIE: Of course, I'm her Aunt Jamie.

EXT./INT. VARIOUS LOCATIONS - DAY/NIGHT
Novels by Rusty Clanton plays over a montage of home video footage of Jamie and Beau living together. Jamie is usually the one filming and Beau is the focus in most of these.

BEGIN MONTAGE:

EXT. JAMIE'S HOUSE - DAY
Beau moves in with Jamie. They sit together on moving boxes. Rearranging the house together.

EXT. JAMIE'S HOUSE - DAY

Setting up picture frames from when they were little to present day.

INT. JAMIE'S HOUSE - DAY

Beau and Jamie struggle to build a crib. Bickering over the instructions. High five when it's done.

INT. JAMIE'S HOUSE - NIGHT

Jamie and Beau help Caroline in the middle of the night. Beau bottle feeds Caroline. Tries to hide from the camera.

INT. JAMIE'S HOUSE - DAY

Jamie and Beau catch Caroline walking.

INT. JAMIE'S HOUSE - NIGHT

Jamie is studying and Beau is sitting next to her reading to Caroline.

EXT. PARK - DAY

Jamie and Beau play with Caroline who is now a toddler. Beau reads to

*Caroline. Jamie, Beau, and Caroline
get in a tickle fight.*

INT. GROCERY STORE - DAY

*Jamie and Beau push Caroline around in
a shopping cart while getting
groceries. Jamie is trying to sneak
junk food into the cart.*

INT. AQUARIUM - DAY

*Beau and Jamie take Caroline to the
aquarium and watch the walrus show.*

INT. JAMIE'S HOUSE - DAY

*Jamie is caught playing princess tea
party with Caroline and Beau joins
them.*

INT. JAMIE'S HOUSE - DAY

*Caroline is giving Beau a makeover
turning him into a cat with whiskers
on his face. Beau laughs and smiles
really big.*

INT. AIRPORT - DAY

Jamie, Beau and Caroline send off Lily at the airport. Hug and wave bye-bye. Watch the plane take off.

INT. JAMIE'S HOUSE - DAY

Jamie, Beau, and Caroline set up a pretend wedding. Jamie walks down the aisle between the guests of teddy bears and other toys. Jamie and Beau almost kiss but get interrupted by Caroline going in the middle. They start kissing her face and laugh. Jamie, Beau, and Caroline dance around.

INT. UNIVERSITY AUDITORIUM - DAY

Jamie graduates. Beau and Caroline cheer from the audience as she walks across the stage.

INT. JAMIE'S HOUSE - NIGHT

Beau carries Jamie to her bed. Beau kisses Jamie's forehead. Filmed by Caroline.

EXT. KID'S RESTAURANT - NIGHT

> *Jamie and Beau celebrate Caroline's 4th birthday. Caroline blows out her candles on her pineapple upside down cake.*

END MONTAGE.

INT. CHURCH - DAY

> *The montage is revealed to have been playing on a projector at the funeral.*

YOUNG ADULT JAMIE: Beau's daughter Caroline was his entire life. And I am grateful to have had them in mine the last few years. My sweet baby girl Caroline was the truest love of Beau's life. I hope everyone in this room finds peace knowing I will do everything as her guardian to make sure she will always know just how much her daddy loves her. You hear me, Caroline? Daddy loves you so so much.

CAROLINE: Daddy loves me past the moon.

YOUNG ADULT JAMIE: Yes, Caroline, past the moon, in all known and unknown universes.

Caroline jumps out of her seat and runs to hug Jamie.

INT. JAMIE'S HOUSE - NIGHT

Beau and Jamie are lying on the floor next to each other while Caroline is playing around them. They are looking at the glow in the dark stars on the ceiling of Caroline's room.

YOUNG ADULT BEAU: Should I even bother going tonight?

YOUNG ADULT JAMIE: Yes, you need to go out.

YOUNG ADULT BEAU: I haven't partied in years. It'll be lame. I should just stay home with you guys.

YOUNG ADULT JAMIE: And do what? Watch 50 first dates again?

YOUNG ADULT BEAU: That would actually be great. Let me go get it.

> *Beau tries to sit up, but Jamie grabs the back of his shirt and pulls him down.*

YOUNG ADULT JAMIE: Do not!

> *Beau turns and lays down facing Jamie.*

YOUNG ADULT BEAU: But really, I'd rather just stay right here with you, on the floor. It's more fun than any party.

YOUNG ADULT JAMIE: Lying on the floor is more fun than a party?

YOUNG ADULT BEAU: With you it is, plus I feel bad leaving you stuck at home with the... *(whispers jokingly)* ...child.

YOUNG ADULT JAMIE: Seriously, go to the party. You deserve a night off! Don't you worry about me and my girl here. We're gonna have a party too. Plus, Lily's coming

over. She's back from London so I'm excited
to see her.

Jamie hugs Caroline.

YOUNG ADULT JAMIE: *(to Caroline)* Right, baby
girl?

Caroline nods.

YOUNG ADULT BEAU: You promise, this is
fine?

YOUNG ADULT JAMIE: Yes, you trust me?

Jamie puts her pinkie up.

YOUNG ADULT BEAU: Yes, I trust you.

*Beau puts his pinkie up and they make
a pinkie promise.*

YOUNG ADULT JAMIE: Go have fun!

YOUNG ADULT BEAU: You guys too.

*Beau kisses his daughter's forehead
and hugs her.*

CAROLINE: Love you, daddy!

YOUNG ADULT BEAU: I love you too, baby.

CAROLINE: To the moon?

YOUNG ADULT BEAU: Past the moon in every
known and unknown universe, baby. As long
as there's stars in the sky, I will love
you.

*Beau kisses her again before putting
her back down.*

YOUNG ADULT BEAU: Okay, I'm going to go
now. Bye bye.

CAROLINE: Bye bye.

YOUNG ADULT JAMIE: Bye.

*Beau goes to close the door, then
opens it again.*

YOUNG ADULT BEAU: Are you "for sure" sure?

YOUNG ADULT JAMIE: Oh my god, go away!

Jamie pushes his hands off the door and shuts it.

YOUNG ADULT JAMIE: Dad's very silly, isn't he, Caroline?

Caroline nods and giggles.

INT. BAR - LATER THAT NIGHT

Beau is dancing and drinking with his friends. Clearly having a good time. Beau spots Ivy from across the room and his smile leaves. Beau walks toward Ivy despite his friends trying to stop him.

YOUNG ADULT BEAU: *(furiously)* Where the hell have you been?

YOUNG ADULT IVY: *(annoyed)* Don't do this.

YOUNG ADULT BEAU: Don't do what? Ask the mother of my child where she's been?

YOUNG ADULT IVY: Can we talk outside? I don't wanna ruin the party.

YOUNG ADULT BEAU: Fine.

INT. JAMIE'S LIVING ROOM

Jamie and Lily are sitting with Beau's teddy bear as Caroline serves them pretend tea.

YOUNG ADULT JAMIE: How was England? Did it rain the entire time?

YOUNG ADULT LILY: No, not that I would know, I spent the entire time in a research lab. You know how it is. But it's good to be back and see you and I'm excited that you'll be joining the I.B.F. team once they start it over here. It's too bad, I'll be going back to England, and we won't be working together. But more importantly, how's this situation going? You and Beau? Are you together yet?

YOUNG ADULT JAMIE: What, no. We're platonic.

YOUNG ADULT LILY: And I'm the Queen of England.

YOUNG ADULT JAMIE: What?

YOUNG ADULT LILY: Oh, come on. Why can't you just accept that you're still in love with him?

YOUNG ADULT JAMIE: Stop it.

YOUNG ADULT LILY: No, I'm serious. You're living together. Raising a kid. Why not go for it?

YOUNG ADULT JAMIE: Because what if I lose him?

YOUNG ADULT LILY: What do you mean? You won't lose him.

YOUNG ADULT JAMIE: When I confessed the first time, I lost him. If I accept that I still love him, in *that way,* I risk losing the friendship we've built over eleven years and then rebuilt during the last three. Over what? Some stupid feelings.

Jamie looks over at Caroline who is playing in her play kitchen.

YOUNG ADULT JAMIE: That's another thing, what about her? What happens if we do get together, and it changes things. What if the pressure of being in love changes the love? There's already love here. And I am so in love with this love. I'm not ever risking it. I have them and I am so happy.

YOUNG ADULT LILY: If that's enough for you.

YOUNG ADULT JAMIE: It is, it really is. I'm happy.

YOUNG ADULT LILY: I know you are.

YOUNG ADULT JAMIE: You know what is making me sad though?

YOUNG ADULT LILY: Oh no, what?

YOUNG ADULT JAMIE: The fact you spent a year and a half in England, and you didn't pick up the accent.

> *Lily and Jamie start laughing.*
> *Caroline runs over and sits in Jamie's lap and hugs her.*

PART ONE, CHAPTER SIX

EXT. BAR PARKING LOT - NIGHT

Beau and Ivy walk out of the bar, and Beau yells at Ivy.

YOUNG ADULT BEAU: Where did you go? You disappeared for four freaking years!

YOUNG ADULT IVY: I went to New York.

YOUNG ADULT BEAU: New York?

YOUNG ADULT IVY: I had to go.

YOUNG ADULT BEAU: *(yelling)* You had to? You had to?

YOUNG ADULT IVY: *(frustrated)* If I knew you were coming to the party, I wouldn't have come. What do you want from me?

YOUNG ADULT BEAU: *(tired)* Can you please just tell me the truth?

YOUNG ADULT IVY: What do you want me to say?

YOUNG ADULT BEAU: The truth?

YOUNG ADULT IVY: And what is that? What is the truth to you, Beau?

YOUNG ADULT BEAU: I loved you.

YOUNG ADULT IVY: And I'm guessing, I didn't love you.

YOUNG ADULT BEAU: Yes, and I knew that the entire time, but it didn't stop me from loving you with my entire being. I gave you everything I had.

YOUNG ADULT IVY: Beau, I loved you the only way I could. I wanted to love you so badly.

YOUNG ADULT BEAU: Wanted? But couldn't?

YOUNG ADULT IVY: *(convincing him)* Beau, listen, I couldn't love you properly, I was messed up, I couldn't love you the way you needed.

YOUNG ADULT BEAU: *(painfully)* The way I needed to be loved was by you. I needed you, Ives. *(Beat.)* Our baby needed her mom. That's it.

YOUNG ADULT IVY: It was never that simple, and you know it.

YOUNG ADULT BEAU: But it *could've* been, if you had tried a little harder, if you held on like you said you would, like you *promised* me. If you stayed and just let me love you, we would've been okay. The three of us, like you promised.

YOUNG ADULT IVY: No, we wouldn't have been, because...

YOUNG ADULT BEAU: Because what? Say it!

YOUNG ADULT IVY: *(tense)* Because you're crazy, okay? We would've never made it because of you.

    Beau is silent.

YOUNG ADULT IVY: *(tired)* Loving you was so tiring; I just couldn't do it anymore. You cried over everything, and got pissed at nothing, it was not okay, I couldn't stay with you, because you were killing me with your "love". You never did anything I wanted to do. I couldn't be myself with you. I was dying.

YOUNG ADULT BEAU: *(heartbroken)* Fuck you.

Ivy puts her head in her hands.

YOUNG ADULT BEAU: I loved you. I gave up everything to love you. I kept choosing you over and over hoping you'd choose me back.

YOUNG ADULT IVY: I never asked you to do any of that! You kept choosing me even when there was no reason to. That was you. Being in love with me was your choice, your decision. I had nothing to do with that. That's the truth. It was all you, Beau!

YOUNG ADULT BEAU: No, you don't get to say that to me. You have no right to say that.

YOUNG ADULT IVY: Let it go, Beau! We've been over for so long, just stop it.

YOUNG ADULT BEAU: I'll stop when you tell me the truth. Please, just give me the truth.

Beau grabs Ivy's arm. She slaps him.

YOUNG ADULT IVY: YOU WANTED THE TRUTH! I TOLD YOU THE TRUTH. LET ME GO.

Ivy hits him over and over until he lets her arm go.

YOUNG ADULT IVY: JUST STOP IT. YOU'RE CRAZY!

YOUNG ADULT BEAU: No, no, no.

YOUNG ADULT IVY: Beau… you have got to listen to me… I'm sorry, I don't know what else to do, I can't keep you, I can't. You can hate me, I made you feel shitty, I made you cry, I called you crazy. Make me the bad guy and let me go. I ran away because I can't do this for you, I know nothing, I can't make you better. And I know I never will. I messed up, I can't do it so you gotta do it, because…

Ivy starts to break down.

YOUNG ADULT IVY: I can't, my love.

Ivy holds Beau's face and then kisses him while they are both crying.

YOUNG ADULT IVY: I can't do it. I can't be who you need me to be. I can't be who she needs me to be. You can. (*Pause.*) You will be everything to her. I know you will. And I'll disappear again, and you both will be better because of it. I promise you, Beau. Just let me go.

Ivy starts to walk away.

YOUNG ADULT BEAU: Caroline looks just like you. Every day, I look at her, and all I see is you. I don't want Caroline growing up wondering where her face came from.

YOUNG ADULT IVY: I wanted it to be you. And I wanted her so badly. I loved every minute of growing her. But the moment I looked into her beautiful brown eyes; I knew I could never become the mom she needs. I left. I'm not going to pretend to be something I can't ever be. I love her so much. I'm giving her the best thing I can. Why can't you understand that? Tell me you understand.

YOUNG ADULT BEAU: I know exactly what you're doing.

YOUNG ADULT IVY: Then tell me.

YOUNG ADULT BEAU: You're running away like your dad did.

Ivy leaves Beau standing there.

PART ONE, CHAPTER SEVEN

INT. CHURCH - DAY

> *As Jamie and Caroline start cleaning up after everyone else leaves, Ivy walks in.*

YOUNG ADULT IVY: Hi, Jamie. Can I talk to you?

> *Jamie kneels to talk to Caroline.*

YOUNG ADULT JAMIE: *(trying to hold it together)* Sweet girl, can you go over there?

CAROLINE: Okay, Auntie J.

> *Caroline goes to help Lily who is cleaning up.*

YOUNG ADULT IVY: She's so big now.

YOUNG ADULT JAMIE: *(quiet rage)* What are you doing here?

YOUNG ADULT IVY: Just wanted to share my condolences.

YOUNG ADULT JAMIE: *(irritated)* You don't know what happened, do you?

YOUNG ADULT IVY: Jamie, I just wanted to come pay my respects. Don't make it a bad thing.

YOUNG ADULT JAMIE: *(assertive)* You should leave now.

> Jamie tries to walk away, Ivy grabs Jamie's arm, stopping her.

YOUNG ADULT IVY: Let me meet her. Please. I just want to meet her.

YOUNG ADULT JAMIE: You thought the best time to meet her would be during her dad's funeral?

YOUNG ADULT IVY: I know the timing is bad, but I want to meet her. She needs her mom. Now more than ever and that's me. I'm her mom. Please, she's my kid.

YOUNG ADULT JAMIE: *(building in anger)* She's not your kid. She stopped being yours when

you left them. When you abandoned your baby
and broke my best friend's heart. When you
left him with nothing. And then you came
back and took some more. They were fine
without you. I had them. I helped him
rebuild everything you broke when you left.
You left them, never forget that.

YOUNG ADULT IVY: I'm sorry, I'm so sorry.

YOUNG ADULT JAMIE: *(tired)* It's too late for
that. Beau is dead. Caroline's almost five.
You missed every opportunity to be a decent
person a long time ago.

Jamie wipes away tears.

YOUNG ADULT JAMIE: He is gone. And she is
not yours. No. She is mine. Mine.

*Jamie starts to cry. Caroline runs
over to comfort her. Caroline gets
upset.*

CAROLINE: *(to Ivy)* You're mean. Go away. You
made Auntie J cry. That's not nice.

Ivy hugs Caroline.

YOUNG ADULT IVY: My sweet girl.

Caroline pushes Ivy away. Ivy keeps holding on as Caroline hits and screams.

CAROLINE: No, no, no. Go away. Go, go, go.

Ivy starts to cry as she lets Caroline go. Ivy stands there clutching her penny necklace watching as Caroline hugs Jamie.

YOUNG ADULT IVY: I really did love them, Jamie. I really did.

Ivy walks away. Ivy realises this is the last time she will see Caroline. Ivy takes one look back before exiting out the church doors.

CAROLINE: It's okay, Aunt Jamie. The mean lady is gone. I love you. I'm here. I got you.

INT. JAMIE'S HOUSE - NIGHT

Beau walks in completely drunk and goes straight to the kitchen and starts rummaging through the drawers ignoring Jamie. Jamie is wearing a wedding dress cleaning up the princess tea party she had with Caroline. Jamie talks to Beau not paying attention to what he is doing as she continues to clean.

YOUNG ADULT JAMIE: Caroline's asleep, she made us dress up and we watched the rainbow princess six times before she passed out, Lily left halfway through the third watch. I don't know if she's gonna come back after that. I can't believe this dress still fits me. And we ate some sandwiches today, did you know Caroline likes them cut in lines? She told me today that foods that are cut up into lines are the best foods, and sorry, what are you looking for?

Beau grabs a knife and goes to the bathroom. Jamie notices him walking by.

YOUNG ADULT JAMIE: Woah, what are you doing with that? Give it to me.

Beau presses the knife with the dull side against his arm.

YOUNG ADULT BEAU: Ivy was there. Did you know that she doesn't love me? No, she just can't love me. No no, what she said was she can't love me the way I need to be loved. What kind of special love am I asking for that makes it impossible for anyone to love me? And she thinks we're better off without her, like her leaving us was some sort of heroic sacrifice. Well, that is bullshit. Bullshit. She grew a baby inside her for nine whole months, and now that she's four years old, she doesn't want her anymore. She used to sing to her stomach. What was that for? Her daughter knows her voice for no reason. She doesn't want her anymore, because of me. She doesn't want me. My daughter doesn't have a mom because of me. She doesn't love me. She can't love me. She can't. That's what she said. Can't, can't, can't. She said she can't love me.

YOUNG ADULT JAMIE: Beau, hand me the knife.

YOUNG ADULT BEAU: It's fine, it's just pressure. It is completely safe as long as I don't move. As long as I don't move, I'll still be okay, it can't hurt me unless *I decide* to move my hand. I am still in control. Jam, just listen to my story.

YOUNG ADULT JAMIE: *(terrified)* Hand me the knife, Beau. *(Beat.)* Please.

YOUNG ADULT BEAU: It's not even the sharp side, it's okay, I know what I'm doing, it's just pressure to feel something, anything other than that, fucking empty bullshit I'm filled with.

> *Beau starts to laugh, takes the knife off his arm as he laughs before finally dropping the knife.*

YOUNG ADULT JAMIE: Why are you laughing?

YOUNG ADULT BEAU: How the hell can I be filled with emptiness? How does that work?

*Jamie realises Beau had cut his arm.
Jamie's eyes fill with tears and panic
as she rushes to grab towels.*

YOUNG ADULT BEAU: Oh shit.

*Beau sits down holding his arm as
blood soaks through the towel on his
arm. Jamie moves the knife away, uses
towels to soak up the blood, and then
calls 911. She holds the phone in
between her shoulder and ear and then
attends to Beau. She rips her dress to
make a tourniquet.*

YOUNG ADULT JAMIE: *(to 911 Operator)* Hello,
yes, my best friend, he's bleeding. There's
so much. *(to Beau)* Beau, I don't know what
to do. There's so much blood. Please don't
die. *(to 911 Operator)* We live near the
hospital. 700 8th Street West. Please
hurry. Please. Please.

*Jamie sits next to him getting blood
on her gown while holding pressure on*

his arm. He keeps bleeding through the towels.

YOUNG ADULT JAMIE: *(calmly but desperate)* Look at me. You made a promise. Remember we die at the same time when we're old. Twenty-one is not old. Not old enough. You aren't allowed to die.

Beau weakly smiles at Jamie.

YOUNG ADULT BEAU: Jam, did you know that I love you.

YOUNG ADULT JAMIE: *(frustrated and scared)* No, no, no, don't do that.

YOUNG ADULT BEAU: *(calmly)* Jamie, just...

Jamie is crying.

YOUNG ADULT BEAU: *(regretfully)* I should've gone with you.

YOUNG ADULT JAMIE: Where? We can go, wherever you want.

YOUNG ADULT BEAU: The dance. It should've been you. *(Beat.)* That would've been nice.

Beau puts his head on Jamie's shoulder.

YOUNG ADULT JAMIE: I won't let you. Please Beau, think about Caroline. Please. Please.

YOUNG ADULT BEAU: *(knowing they're his last words)* I love her. I love her so much. Tell her that. Take care of her. Prom... Promise me. You'll pro..tect her. Do whatever you have to. Please.

Beau weakly raises his other hand trying to make a pinkie promise. Jamie just meets his hand where it is and completes the promise.

YOUNG ADULT JAMIE: I promise.

Jamie nods and rests her head on Beau's.

YOUNG ADULT JAMIE: I love you, Beau. Please just stay with me.

> *Jamie continues to hold Beau as Caroline walks in. Beau's breathing has slowed, his hand loosened, and he is no longer responsive.*

YOUNG ADULT JAMIE: *(begging)* Oh god, go back to bed sweetheart, please go back to bed.

CAROLINE: *(innocently confused)* Why is daddy sleeping in the bathroom?

YOUNG ADULT JAMIE: *(calmly)* It's okay, you just go back to sleep.

> *Caroline goes to give Beau a good night kiss as blue and red lights flash in the small window above them. Caroline does not pay attention to the blood now covering her princess dress. She softly hums her lullaby, only stopping when the medics come in and take Beau's body away.*

CAROLINE: Is daddy going to get a band-aid?

Jamie picks Caroline up. Both are covered in Beau's blood.

YOUNG ADULT JAMIE: *(trying to convince herself)* Yes, daddy's gonna get a band-aid. He will be okay. And you will be okay. We will all be okay.

Jamie and Caroline go in the ambulance with Beau.

CAROLINE: *(reassuring)* Don't cry, it's just a band-aid.

Jamie smiles as she remembers something.

EXT. SUBURBAN STREET - DAY

Jamie watches Beau attempt to bike down the hill.

CHILD BEAU: I'M GOING SO FAST! JAMIE! YOU'RE GOING TO REMEMBER THIS FOREVER! THE BRILLIANT BEAU! REMEMBER ME FOREVER!

INT. HOSPITAL WAITING ROOM - NIGHT

Caroline sits in Jamie's lap in a near empty waiting room.

CAROLINE: Can you finish the song?

YOUNG ADULT JAMIE: For you, baby girl, I'd do anything. But I can't sing right now because we have to be quiet in hospitals, so is it okay if I hum it very quietly?

Caroline nods her head. Jamie starts to hum the song as Caroline melts into her.

EXT. BEACH - DAY

Child Beau and Child Jamie stand at Beau's mom's funeral. Child Beau cries and Child Jamie hugs him.

CHILD BEAU: Thanks for being here.

CHILD JAMIE: I'll always be here.

INT. HOSPITAL - DAY

> *Jamie holds a sleeping Caroline in her arms as the doctor comes out to talk to her.*

DOCTOR: Are you the family of Robert Arden?

YOUNG ADULT JAMIE: Yes, is he okay?

DOCTOR: Follow me, we can talk here.

> *The doctor leads Jamie to a small empty room with just a table and a few chairs. As she nervously sits down, Jamie asks:*

YOUNG ADULT JAMIE: He's not okay, is he?

DOCTOR: When he arrived, he had already lost quite a large amount of blood. His injury was severe as the cephalic vein, a major blood vessel in his left arm, had been cut. Despite our best efforts, due to his blood condition, we could not stop the bleeding. I'm sorry to tell you that Robert-

YOUNG ADULT JAMIE: Beau. He prefers Beau.

DOCTOR: I'm sorry, Beau has died. I'm sorry for your loss.

> *Jamie starts to tear up but does not let herself cry. She kisses the top of Caroline's head. The doctor leaves.*

EXT. BEACH - SUNSET

> *Jamie holds Caroline in her arms as they toss Beau's ashes into the ocean. Afterwards, Jamie stands frozen as the other guests say their goodbyes until it is just her and Caroline left. For a moment, there is peace as the sun begins to set.*

> *Lily comes and takes the now sleeping four-year-old from Jamie's tired arms. As Lily walks toward the lone car in the distance, Jamie takes her sandals off and runs into the water. She shouts and screams and sobs while fighting against the weight of the soaked dress she is wearing. Lily*

*turns around and watches from the
shore still holding the sleeping
Caroline. Jamie lets out one last
painfully guttural scream before
falling to her knees and crawling back
to shore. She sits facing the ocean as
the sunlight disappears and darkness
surrounds her.*

YOUNG ADULT JAMIE: *(under her breath)* You
were mine. And I was yours. That could've
been enough. *(Beat.)* Why couldn't that have
been enough?

PART TWO: HER

PART TWO, CHAPTER ONE

INT. HOSPITAL - MORNING

IVY, a 22-year-old woman, sits and eats breakfast with her mom who is sitting up in a hospital bed.

IVY'S MOM: Thanks for being here, baby.

IVY: No worries, mom.

IVY'S MOM: How was Allie's birthday?

IVY: I saw Beau.

IVY'S MOM: Oh? How is he?

Ivy considers what to say next.

IVY: I didn't get a chance to talk to him; he was leaving when I got there.

IVY'S MOM: *(knows Ivy is lying)* Okay. Well, did he look happy?

IVY: *(continuing to lie)* Yeah, he did.

INT. POST OFFICE - DAY

> *Ivy gets her mail and then sorts them at the recycle bin. She looks at the corkboard on the wall nearby and sees an obituary that she can't help but memorise. She drops her mail as her breathing increases.*

ROBERT "BEAU" ARDEN, 21,
DIED JUNE 30TH
WILL BE FOREVER MISSED BY
HIS DAUGHTER CAROLINE ARDEN
FUNERAL SERVICE WILL BE HELD
ON JULY 9TH AT HOLY MISSION CHURCH

> *She quickly picks her mail off the floor and rushes out the door.*

EXT. OUTSIDE THE POST OFFICE

> *Ivy rushes down the stairs and gets into her car. She begins violently sobbing.*

INT. IVY'S CAR

> *Ivy calls AUDREY, her older sister, on speaker phone and tells her:*

IVY: Beau died.

AUDREY: What?

IVY: He died.

AUDREY: How?

IVY: I don't know. I just saw his obit at the post office, I was just getting my mail, and I looked up and... He's dead. It said his funeral is in a week.

AUDREY: Are you going to go?

IVY: I don't know what to do. (Beat.) Do you think Caroline's okay?

AUDREY: I hope so. Where are you? I'll drive us home. I'll get a taxi, and I'll drive your car, okay?

IVY: Okay, I'm outside the post office. But can we go see mom before home?

AUDREY: Okay, I'll be there in a bit.

INT. HIGH SCHOOL GYM - NIGHT

Ivy is sitting at a table with her friends at a school dance. Beau whispers something to ALLIE, his school friend, who immediately runs to tell Ivy.

ALLIE: Oh my god, Beau just told me the cutest thing. Ivy, he has a crush on you.

Beau is embarrassed, but Ivy smiles at him.

IVY: Aw, thanks. You wanna join us?

BEAU: No, it's okay... I don't want to bother you, sorry.

IVY: Never a bother. Anyone who has a crush on me is welcome here. I appreciate the compliment. Here.

Ivy pats the spot next to her. Beau sits down.

IVY: Welcome, Kid. We'll take care of you tonight; we'll have some fun.

BEAU: Okay.

IVY: How have we never hung out? We're in the same grade.

BEAU: You're cool and I'm me.

IVY: *(whispering to Beau)* If you want, I'll give you my number and we can hangout sometime. Just don't tell the others. It can be our thing. You and me.

BEAU: You and me, okay.

> *The music changes and all the other people at the table get up to dance. Ivy gets Beau to join them. They dance all together. Ivy pulls Beau away to the speakers.*

IVY: Put your hand here.

> *Ivy places Beau's hand on the speaker.*

IVY: Just feel it.

Ivy and Beau look at each other while feeling the music. They smile at each other.

EXT. OUTSIDE THE POST OFFICE
Ivy is sitting in her car. There is a knock on the window, Ivy gets out of the car and hugs Audrey.

AUDREY: Hey, I got you. I got you.

Ivy just collapses into her and just cries.

EXT. PARK - NIGHT
Ivy and Beau sit on a middle school playground structure.

IVY: Austin broke up with me today at lunch.

BEAU: Yeah, I heard about that. I feel bad.

IVY: You weren't the reason.

Beau doesn't say anything.

IVY: He was just done with me.

BEAU: Are you doing okay?

IVY: Yeah, I'm okay. I guess this means we can say the things we want to say now. (Beat.) And do the things we want to do.

Beau stands up and walks away from Ivy. He looks up at the sky and sees a heart in the stars. Ivy stands up and starts to walk over to him. Beau closes his eyes and takes a breath before turning around.

IVY: Hey, you okay?

Beau kisses Ivy for the first time.

IVY: Cool.

BEAU: Ivy, I love you.

IVY: That's a mistake.

BEAU: Ives, I'm serious.

IVY: I am too.

> *A car pulls up to the park. Beau's dad yells from inside.*

BEAU'S DAD: Beau! Get your ass in this car right now!

BEAU: *(to Ivy)* Sorry.

> *Beau runs to the car and gets in. Ivy is left sitting alone in the dark.*

IVY: I think I do love you. I'm sorry.

INT. HOSPITAL - NIGHT
> *Ivy sits at her mom's bedside. Audrey stands by the door.*

IVY: I talked to him last week. I yelled at him. I hit him. I broke his heart. The last conversation we had was that. What if… what if he did something because of...

IVY'S MOM: Ivy, don't.

IVY: But, mom, he died that night. That night.

IVY'S MOM: Anything that happened, you weren't part of it. You weren't there. You don't even know what happened.

IVY: I'm a bad person.

IVY'S MOM: No, you are not. You are my daughter.

Ivy breaks and starts crying again.

EXT. IVY'S HOUSE - MORNING
Ivy drives up to her old house and gets out of the car and looks down the road and remembers:

EXT. IVY'S HOUSE - AFTERNOON
7-year-old Ivy runs after a car driving away. Her mom and sister

follow her. All of them are crying as Ivy screams:

IVY: Come back. Don't leave me! I love you. Come back! Come back! Daddy, take me with you! I'll be good. I promise.

Ivy keeps running. She loses one of her flip flops, before tripping on the other one folding. She scrapes her knee and sits in the middle of the street crying as she watches the car drive away.

INT. IVY'S HOUSE - MORNING

Ivy walks inside the house into the kitchen where another memory resurfaces.

10-year-old Ivy sits on the steps of the stairs listening to her mom and Audrey argue downstairs.

IVY'S MOM: WHAT DO YOU NEED ME TO DO? YOU WANT ME TO STAY HOME WITH YOU ALL DAY, EVERYDAY? YOU DON'T WANT ME TO WORK. JUST

TAKE CARE OF YOU. I CAN'T DO THAT. I HAVE
TO WORK. I HAVE TO PUT FOOD ON THE TABLE
FOR YOU AND YOUR SISTER.

YOUNG AUDREY: I JUST NEED YOU TO BE HERE
FOR ME.

IVY'S MOM: HOW? TELL ME HOW?

YOUNG AUDREY: I DON'T KNOW.

IVY'S MOM: WHY DO YOU DO THIS?

YOUNG AUDREY: I DON'T KNOW! WHY CAN'T YOU
UNDERSTAND?

IVY'S MOM: YOU WANT ME TO UNDERSTAND. I'LL
UNDERSTAND.

> *Young Ivy runs down the stairs and
> peeks into the kitchen through the
> kitchen door trying not to be seen.
> Ivy's mom is holding a knife to her
> own neck.*

YOUNG AUDREY: NO, MOM, STOP IT.

IVY'S MOM: WHY DON'T WE BOTH JUST GET IT OVER WITH TONIGHT? IS THAT WHAT YOU WANT?

All three of them are crying now. The yelling has turned into begging.

YOUNG AUDREY: No, mom, please stop. I'll stop, I'll stop.

Ivy's mom lowers the knife as Audrey falls to her knees begging her to stop.

IVY'S MOM: If you die, I die. And where will Ivy go if we're not here? I need you here. I love you. I only have you girls. There's no one else.

Young Ivy watches as her mom and sister hold each other on the kitchen floor.

INT. IVY'S HOUSE - MORNING
Ivy goes to her old bedroom:

INT. IVY'S HOUSE - NIGHT

14-year-old Ivy is asleep when her mom crawls into her bed. Ivy wakes up when her mom kisses her forehead.

IVY: Mom? What are you doing?

IVY'S MOM: Ivy baby, she left. It's just us now. Promise me something.

IVY: Anything.

IVY'S MOM: Don't leave me alone. You're my last hope, my baby.

Ivy wraps herself around her mom. Her mom sobs in Ivy's arms. Ivy joins her in crying.

INT. IVY'S HOUSE - MORNING
22-year-old Ivy runs out of the house to the backyard where she looks down the back alley:

EXT. BACK ALLEY - NIGHT
16-year-old Beau and 17-year-old Ivy walking together.

BEAU: You really didn't know?

Beau laughs loudly with a snort.

IVY: Don't laugh at me. How was I supposed to know?

BEAU: I just don't know how you could listen to it and not know that it's a metaphor.

IVY: Okay, well, it sounds like a guy being possessive of his girlfriend.

BEAU: That's the point.

IVY: Whatever, thanks for just pointing out how stupid I am. It feels amazing.

BEAU: Ives, I'm sorry, you know I think you're incredible. I wrote something for you last night.

IVY: I am going to sing this out loud, is that okay? You got to tell me if I'm doing it right.

Beau nods.

IVY: To the sun/Lovely and lonely/With no one to see/Run away, run away, run away/We'll get out of this town/I promise, we'll take off/And never come back/Say goodbye/to the snow/and the storms/And empty houses/We'll never return to/We'll never return to

BEAU: So? What do you think?

IVY: I think it could make an awesome song.

BEAU: Only if you sing it.

IVY: I need you to write me some songs to sing.

BEAU: And I need you to write your autograph on something I own before it costs a thousand dollars.

IVY: You're too kind, dear sir.

BEAU: You are deserving, your highness.

IVY: Would you run away with me?

BEAU: Right now? Yes.

IVY: No, not now, but hypothetically, would you?

BEAU: I'd follow you to the ends of the earth, no doubt about it, Ives.

IVY: This is why I love you. I asked Austin that last night when we were texting, and he said it was dumb cause I can just move out once we graduate, but like no, there's no adventure in that, you get it, kid. You know what I mean. You understand me. He just doesn't get me like you do.

BEAU: We're soulmates, and one day we'll find out what we're meant to be. I'll be a kick ass writer, and you'll be selling records like crazy.

IVY: I can see us, I'm doing my acceptance speech for some kind of award, and I point you out in the audience as everyone claps.

I've made it with you by my side and it's amazing.

BEAU: You're amazing.

IVY: I am pretty amazing, aren't I?

BEAU: Don't forget about me when you're lounging in your penthouse apartment in New York City one day.

IVY: I won't forget you because you'll be right there with me.

BEAU: Sounds like a plan. *(Beat.)* But what is this? Like I love you, but am I allowed to? You're still with Austin. If he's your boyfriend, what am I?

IVY: I know, I'm sorry it's so confusing. Here, how can I make it make sense? You're my forever, Austin's just a high school sweetheart. It'll be you when you're ready. I know you made a promise to your mom to wait till you're done with high school to date. I respect it. I don't understand it.

But I respect it. *(Beat.)* Austin's nice, he just never hangs out with me. But I don't know, it just makes sense to keep him around for now. I mean, you'll get me for the rest of time, he can have me for now, that's fair, right, kid?

BEAU: I guess.

> *17-year-old Ivy holds his hand, and they keep walking.*

EXT. IVY'S BACKYARD - MORNING
> *22-year-old Ivy has a guilty look on her face before she turns around and heads back to her house. Her sister is at the door.*

INT. IVY'S BEDROOM - DAY
> *Ivy is trying on different black dresses in her mirror. Audrey is helping.*

IVY: What would you wear to your dead baby daddy's funeral?

AUDREY: You can't say that.

IVY: Okay, what would you wear to the funeral of your ex-boyfriend you got in a fight with and whose heart you broke earlier the night he died?

> *Audrey quietly just wraps her arms around Ivy.*

AUDREY: You didn't kill him. I know you feel like you did, but you didn't.

> *Audrey looks her in the eyes.*

AUDREY: You didn't.

INT. IVY'S BEDROOM - NIGHT

> *Teen Ivy is trying on her dresses for the dance. She is wearing a tight-fitting red dress. Her door is open, and her mom walks by and stops.*

IVY'S MOM: Ivy, are you sure you want to wear that one?

IVY: What's wrong?

IVY'S MOM: Your stomach. It's too tight, wear the blue one. The flowy one. It'll hide it. You'll look nicer. Prettier. Sexier.

IVY: You mean thinner.

IVY'S MOM: What?

IVY: You say sexier, I know you mean thinner. *(Beat.)* I'm allowed to have a stomach. And so are you.

> *Ivy's mom leaves. Ivy shuts her door. Ivy takes off the red dress and takes the blue one out. She doesn't put it on; she just holds it as she looks at herself in the mirror.*

INT. IVY'S BEDROOM - NIGHT

> *It is the night of the dance. Beau and Ivy lay next to each other naked under Ivy's blankets. The muffled sounds of*

BEAU: What's on your mind, love?

IVY: Do you ever think about dying?

BEAU: Yeah, maybe more than I should, why?

IVY: Death is one of those things that fascinates me. I mean, we just stop existing. And it could be an accident, illness, old age or at the hands of someone else. *(Beat.)* Do you think there's a heaven?

BEAU: I don't know. I don't think I believe in that kind of afterlife. I like to think that if there is a heaven, it's more like a waiting room until they have your next life ready for you. I guess I like reincarnation if I had to choose one.

IVY: So, you believe that we come back as something else?

BEAU: Yeah, but I also love the idea of all the different universes existing altogether, so I don't think we come back to the same one all the time. I think even if we die in this reality, there's other versions of us still living their lives in the other universes.

IVY: I like that.

BEAU: This is sad and kinda dark but after my mom died, it was the only way to survive. To just think that she's out there somewhere. She used to tell me when she started to get really sick that she'd be watching me from the moon. But only during the full moons would the windows from the other universes be open, so she'd be there waiting to hear from me. I know it isn't real, but it's still nice to believe. So, every full moon, I go to hospital hill park and sit with her.

IVY: You're so amazing, did you know that? The way your mind works is just so cool to me. I love that you feel so deeply. I love

your brain and no matter how dark or scary
you think it is, I'll love it.

BEAU: Promise?

IVY: I do. I promise.

BEAU: You are so beautiful, Ives.

IVY: Thanks, kid. You are too.

They kiss.

PART TWO, CHAPTER TWO

INT. LOUNGE - AFTERNOON

Ivy and the band are rehearsing. There is flirtation and clear chemistry between Ivy and Kai. Beau walks in with Caroline. He watches them, the other band members see him, but not Kai and Ivy, so the flirtation continues. They finish the song and Beau claps; Ivy and Kai separate from each other. Ivy jumps down and hugs Beau and kisses Caroline.

IVY: Love, you're early. We aren't done till five.

BEAU: I know, I just thought I'd catch the end of it because I never get to watch you perform anymore. You're still absolutely amazing, Ives. *(to the rest of the band)* You're all still absolutely awesome.

KAI: Thanks, man. I think we're just thankful this lovely lady did what she did. I mean, who else but Ivy would not only convince the band to get back together and then also convince her boss to take us all in.

IVY: *(to the band)* Hey, I made the band, of course, I wanted to work with you guys again. I mean, I only stopped because this guy got me pregnant, but I'm back, so the band's back. *(to Beau)* Anyway, we gotta clean up, so are you good waiting a bit, Beau?

BEAU: Yeah, no worries.

> *Ivy kisses his cheek and goes to help. She slightly trips over the mic's cord. Beau goes to catch her despite being too far away. Kai catches her by wrapping his arm around her waist. They giggle together about it. There is a deeper intimacy clear within this small interaction. Caroline starts to cry. Beau sits down and starts rocking Caroline's stroller, his grip tightens on the handle as he continues to watch them interact.*

INT. IVY'S LIVING ROOM - NIGHT

> *Ivy and Audrey are drinking wine and talking on the floor in front of the couch.*

IVY: I feel like a montage, like everything is happening, after another. And I don't really exist; it's just a bunch of moments. Like the past, the future, just got so scrambled inside me. And I feel like running, I'm running as fast as I can. But I don't know what direction I'm going. Audrey puts her head on Ivy's shoulder.

IVY: Am I a bad person? Was Beau right? Am I unforgivable? I just wish I could take it all back. You know, I don't even know why I did any of it. But if I had stayed, it would've been worse. I was unhappy and it wasn't fair to him or to her.

AUDREY: You did what you thought was right when it was happening. For Christ's sake, you were 18 when you had that baby. You didn't leave her in a garbage bag behind a bar; you left her with her dad.

IVY: When did you get so wise?

AUDREY: You fuck up enough times and hurt enough people. You can't help but learn about the world as it turns around to teach you to be better. You loved them. But love isn't enough sometimes.

IVY: I loved them so much, but I knew they'd be better off without me there. *(Beat.)* I guess I was right. He only died after I came back.

AUDREY: Ives...

Ivy takes a big swig of wine straight from the bottle.

INT. IVY'S DINING ROOM - NIGHT

Ivy and Beau are eating supper. Beau watches as Ivy texts someone and smiles to herself.

BEAU: What's so funny?

IVY: Nothing.

BEAU: Did I ever tell you about the time I wrote a love letter to my crush in grade five?

BEAU: Well, I had a crush on this girl since Grade Three, and I thought I should tell her, through a letter. And I told her how I've loved her for so long, and what I love about her, and how I wish I could date her, but here's the best part. *(Pause.)* I ended it by explaining I can't date her because of the promise I made to my mom, you know about that. But anyway, she didn't like me, and she lit that letter on fire and then threw it in a puddle and then stomped on it. Even after that, I still had a crush on her for the next few years. After the letter incident, I told Jamie "I swear to never love someone like that ever again" and it was true, I didn't, until I met you. It sounds so stupid, but I really did love her. I spent years scared to actually love someone because if that silly crush hurt me like that, what would happen when it's real and it's still not enough? (Beat.) I found this recipe online, what do you think? Did I do good?

IVY: Yeah, it's good.

> *Beau gives up and just continues to eat his supper in silence as he listens to Ivy giggle and text. She finishes eating and leaves.*

IVY: I'm going to bed now.

BEAU: Okay, I'll just clean up and I'll join you.

IVY: Okay.

> *Beau starts to clean up. While he does the dishes, he accidentally drops a glass on the floor. He cuts his finger while cleaning it up. He looks in every drawer for a band-aid, he grabs*

a paper towel to wrap around his bleeding finger before heading up the stairs to look in the second-floor bathroom. As he walks past Ivy's bedroom, he overhears her say:

IVY: *(from the other room)* No, no. He just doesn't get it, I mean… He'll never understand me like you do.

Beau keeps walking and starts to cry once he gets in the bathroom. He puts a band-aid on his finger. He looks at himself in the mirror and sighs painfully.

INT. LOUNGE - NIGHT

Ivy is performing and she is a powerhouse. Not a breath in the audience. She finishes the song and heads to the band dressing room, where they talk about the set, afterwards, Ivy and KAI, the guitarist, are left alone.

KAI: Ivy, can we talk?

IVY: Hey yeah, what's up?

KAI: What's going on with us?

IVY: I care about you, I do.

KAI: Yeah, but you're with Beau. And you guys have a kid. What are you doing with me? Beau's so sweet and nice, he's so in love with you, it kills me when he picks you up and I have to pretend there isn't something here. So, tell me, what is this?

IVY: I can't talk about this right now, I'm sorry, just... stop it. Yes, I have feelings for you. Yes, I'm with Beau. But I do care about you, Kai.

KAI: No.

IVY: What do you mean "no"?

KAI: I'm not letting you lead me on anymore. It used to be fun, but I-I can't believe...

IVY: Believe what?

KAI: I actually let myself fall in love with you. I can't be that person. Beau's a friend. I mean, seriously, he's got years with me before you. This is gonna hurt him so bad, Ivy.

IVY: Don't tell him.

KAI: I'm not lying to Beau.

IVY: I'm not asking you to lie, just don't tell him.

KAI: Ivy, how do you keep getting away with this?

IVY: I'm not doing anything, it's not my fault, everyone I hurt keeps letting me hurt them. I hate myself; you hate me, do you really need Beau to hate me too?

KAI: I'm done.

IVY: What do you mean, you're done?

KAI: I mean that I am done. I am done with you.

Kai walks out.

INT. IVY'S LIVING ROOM - NIGHT

Ivy comes home intoxicated in the middle of the night. Beau is asleep on the couch with Caroline sleeping next to him. She sits on the coffee table and just stares at them longingly. She tears up but wipes them away. She adjusts the blanket on Beau before taking Caroline upstairs.

INT. IVY'S BEDROOM - NIGHT

Ivy comes in carrying her sleeping baby and gently places her in her crib beside the bed. She slowly picks out pyjamas for herself and lays them nicely on the bed. She goes to the bathroom.

INT. IVY'S BATHROOM - NIGHT

Ivy slowly undresses and steps into the shower. She turns the water on, sits down, and just stays under the water. Her expression is flat and numb. Caroline begins to cry from the bedroom. Ivy covers her ears with her hands and rocks herself back and forth until the crying stops. Beau opens the shower curtain and immediately jumps in to hold Ivy who is still rocking.

BEAU: Ives, I got you. I got you, I'm here. I'm here now.

IVY: I don't want you.

Ivy is frustrated and weeping now.

BEAU: I know, but I'm here. I'm here. Love, just breathe, my love, breathe.

Ivy leans into him crying and weakly hitting him.

BEAU: I'm glad you're home now. I love you, Ives. I missed you.

Beau kisses her forehead.

PART TWO, CHAPTER THREE

EXT. PARK - DAY

> *Ivy and her band are setting up for their set at a fundraiser. Kai is avoiding Ivy. Beau is watching in the audience with Caroline in her stroller.*

IVY: Kai, thanks for showing up.

KAI: Don't. Let's just get this over with.

> *Ivy goes up to the mic.*

IVY: Hello, everybody. We are Ivy and the Vines, and we are very honoured to be singing here. This is our first performance for this size of audience, usually you'll find us in the Dark Lounge at the Quinton hotel, rocking out to about 20ish people night after night. We hope we can put on a good show for you. Thank you again, all of you beautiful people for helping us make our dreams come true. Here we go!

> *Beau is watching in the crowd and overhears a conversation.*

RANDOM GIRL 1: Apparently, the singer was dating the guitarist, but it ended badly.

RANDOM GIRL 2: What? And they're still in the band together.

RANDOM GIRL 1: My mom works at the hotel they play at, and she overheard a fight from their dressing room.

RANDOM GIRL 2: Well, did she find out why they broke up?

RANDOM GIRL 1: She has a boyfriend, who she has a baby with, and the guitarist was done being used.

RANDOM GIRL 2: Dang, that's gross. But like go off, that guitarist is hot. I wonder what the other guy looks like, probably not as hot as that guy.

The girls laugh. Caroline starts to cry, and the girls look at Beau. They realise who he is and awkwardly walk away. Beau soothes Caroline and

*himself, still trying to process what
the girls were saying.*

BEAU: Shh shh, it's okay, my girl.

*Caroline doesn't stop. Ivy watches as
Beau leaves.*

EXT. PARK PARKING LOT - DAY
*The band is packing up the van. Beau
is rocking Caroline.*

KAI: Hey, Beau. You wanna drive back with
me? Ivy shoved a bunch of stuff in your car
and Caroline won't be comfy in the back and
she's hasn't been having the best day, huh?

BEAU: Yeah, that'd be good, I didn't even
realise she was gonna fill our car. She
didn't tell me.

KAI: She doesn't tell you a lot of things,
huh?

INT. KAI'S CAR - DAY

Kai and Beau drive back to town, just the two of them in the car, with Caroline asleep in the back.

KAI: First things first, I just wanted to say, I'm really glad we reconnected these last few months. I'm sorry, my mom stopped letting me come over after your mom passed away. I didn't understand it fully back then and I should've been a better friend to you. And as your friend, I hate the conversation we are about to have.

BEAU: You fell in love with her, didn't you?

KAI: I genuinely never saw it coming, and I stopped it out of respect for you. It's so shit, because when she and I had that conversation about not taking those feelings any further, I thought she'd at least realise what she did, but I swear it felt like the next day, she was telling me about her feelings about Quincy. I deserve

better than that. It was like I was nothing
to her.

BEAU: It's what she does. She's Ivy and
this is what she does. I mean, you know. I
would've left, but she's my baby's mom.

KAI: You don't have to stay though;
couldn't you take Caroline and go?

BEAU: Kai, you know, I haven't had a mom
since I was 11 and my dad is who knows
where. Ivy's dad left her when she was 7. I
don't want my kid to be anything close to
us. I want Caroline to be able to draw a
proper family photo, two parents holding
her hands. I know all about Ivy's habit of
falling in love with a new and exciting
person every month. I sit and watch and
wait for her to come home and lie to my
face about where she's been. I still set
her a place at the table, even when she
hasn't been home for a few days. When you
love someone like Ivy, hope is a
requirement. I have thought about leaving
and letting go, over and over. I've knelt

before her crying my eyes out begging her
to make a choice about me. She begged me to
just leave. But I refuse. Because I'm not
making my daughter grow up without a
mother. I mean, she's already barely there,
I don't want to think of what would happen
if we didn't live in the same house.

KAI: How does she get away with doing this?
It feels like every time she talks to me
about literally anything, I just want to
die because it hurts. It hurts even worse
to watch her talk to someone else. I'm so
sorry for putting you through that. You
really don't understand till you're in that
position. I should've stopped it before it
even started. I feel like such a shitty
person for putting you in that spot. I'm
just so sorry.

BEAU: You're not the one who needs to
apologise to me. You're still my friend,
and I'm sorry you fell for her too.

KAI: Beau, we'll be okay, right? God, I hope you figure out how to leave, you deserve so much better.

BEAU: I know, but if I don't stay, who will?

INT. IVY'S DINING ROOM - DAY
Ivy's waiting at the dining table when Beau walks in with Caroline and makes his way upstairs to put Caroline in her crib.

IVY: Did Kai talk to you about me?

BEAU: Yup.

Ivy puts her head in her hands before getting up and following Beau upstairs.

INT. IVY'S BEDROOM - AFTERNOON
Ivy walks in as Beau is putting Caroline in her crib.

IVY: What did they tell you?

BEAU: What do you think we talked about?

IVY: Beau, I'm sorry.

BEAU: Do you know what that means? You say it a lot, but do you really understand them?

> *Beau leaves the bedroom and goes downstairs. Ivy follows.*

IVY: I am sorry. I love you, Beau.

BEAU: There's another one, "love", tell me what that word means to you, Ives?

IVY: I don't know what to do.

BEAU: Stop doing this.

IVY: I can't help it. I can't stop feeling.

BEAU: But you know what you can do. You can stop talking to people when you're still with me. God, I should've listened to everyone and ran when I could've. What

would've happened if I just left you when I
wanted to?

IVY: You wanted to leave me?

BEAU: I love you, Ives, but you don't make
it easy some days. I'm staying and I'm
never gonna leave you alone. I just
couldn't do that now. This love is hard and
heavy, but it's you and me, and I made a
promise to you. Even if you don't keep
yours, I keep mine. I'll always be in love
with you, no matter what you do. No matter
how many times you hurt me, or cheat on me,
or you don't love me back.

IVY: I do love you, Beau.

BEAU: I don't think you do. Maybe before,
but not anymore. Just please, could you
just, even just once, *prove me wrong*.

IVY: I didn't do anything with Kai, just by
the way. Don't make it more dramatic than
it needs to be. I never cheated on you.
That I promise. I just fell in love.

BEAU: Isn't that what you said when we started?

IVY: It's different.

BEAU: It's not though.

IVY: I didn't do anything to you, why are you mad? I come home to you, I have a kid with you, what else do you need from me?

BEAU: I want you to love me, Ives. You don't love me.

Ivy walks away as Beau bends down to get a pan from a lower cabinet.

BEAU: You never did.

Beau stands up as Ivy walks out the front door. She slams the door, and Beau continues to prepare supper. He picks up a knife and holds its dull side against his arm until it leaves an impression. He takes a breath and continues to prepare supper.

EXT. IVY'S HOUSE - AFTERNOON

> *Ivy takes a walk and thinks back to another conversation.*

EXT. BEHIND THE HIGH SCHOOL - DAY

> *Austin and Ivy are talking behind the school.*

AUSTIN: Ivy, you don't talk to me anymore. Do you even care about me? Do you even love me?

IVY: Austin, come on, of course I do.

AUSTIN: I think it's time to let us go.

IVY: What are you talking about?

AUSTIN: I'm breaking up with you, Ivy. I'm done waiting around for you. You never hang out with me, you're always busy with everyone else, especially Beau. You know, he's in love with you, right? God, I hope you figure it out, you can't just keep doing whatever you want. You're gonna keep hurting the people who want to love you,

and I'm scared that you're going to find
that out too late.

EXT. IVY'S HOUSE - NIGHT

*Ivy rubs her eyes and takes a breath
walking toward the front door of her
house. She pauses before turning the
doorknob.*

INT. IVY'S HOUSE - NIGHT

*Ivy walks in expecting Beau, but her
mom is sitting there at the table.*

IVY: Where is he?

IVY'S MOM: I don't know. I was going to ask
you. I came home and he asked me to watch
the baby.

IVY: He didn't take Caroline with him?

IVY'S MOM: Why, what's wrong?

*Ivy's phone dings. It's a text from
Beau.*

BEAU (TEXT): Ivy, I'll just lay here under the sky and let it take me away. You don't have to worry about hurting me anymore.

IVY: Mom, I gotta go get him.

IVY'S MOM: Did he say where he is?

IVY: No, but I know where he is.

EXT. HOSPITAL HILL - NIGHT
Ivy runs toward the silhouette of a person sitting in the field. It's Beau. Once she gets to him, Ivy begins to yell at him.

IVY: Don't do this shit. You need serious professional help; this is toxic and manipulative. I thought you were dead. Get the hell up and get in the car. You're not doing this to me.

Beau just stares ahead.

IVY: Beau, get the fuck up. I'm not doing this. You get your shit together. Don't

play this card. Don't victimise yourself.
You know exactly what you're doing. It's
not going to work with me. Get up.

*Ivy pulls him up, but he stays on the
ground. Ivy smacks him on the head.*

IVY: Get up. Get up. Get. The. Fuck. Up.
(Beat.) Fuck you, Beau. I'm not playing
into your pity party. Your daughter is at
home safe, if you come back, good, if not,
whatever. I can't with you, with all the
dramatics. I mean, come on, what was that
text message? What? You want me to care
about you? So, you do this? But you aren't
gonna do anything? You won't. I know you
won't. So, get up and get in the car, you
fucking crazy asshole.

Beau finally looks up at her.

BEAU: *(calmly)* Today, Kai told me to leave
you. I came out here to do some reflecting
before having a conversation with you about
it all. Sorry for the text, I was so out of
it when I wrote it, but I didn't mean

anything bad. I just don't want to be here, in this place with you. I wish I could have the sky take me away somewhere else, but it won't. It can't take me away from you. *(Beat.)* But I can. I will walk away from you for real if I find myself in this situation again. I love you. And I never want to leave you. But sitting here, with the moon, thinking about *everything*, I know that I never want to leave myself. And I feel myself leaving who I am behind in favour of who you want me to be. The problem is, you don't want me to be anything, because you don't want me.

> *Beau finally lifts his head and makes eye contact with Ivy.*

BEAU: So, I'll be whatever you need me to be, just so I can stay. I want to stay. Because I love you, Ivy. I love you so much, and I can't do anything else other than love you. I've tried to hate you. I've tried to copy you. Follow your lead, see if maybe someone else could make up for what you refuse to show me, you know, some of

the girls at work are really nice to me,
but I can't feel anything like this with
anyone else. It's you and me. For me, it's
always you and me.

PART TWO, CHAPTER FOUR

INT. IVY'S BEDROOM - NIGHT

19-year-old Ivy is sitting booking plane tickets to New York. She looks at the baby sleeping next to her.

INT. IVY'S BATHROOM - NIGHT

18-year-old Ivy sits waiting for the timer on her phone to go off. It rings. She picks up the test and counts the lines. She places it next to two other positive tests.

IVY: Okay. So, this is really it. I'm going to be someone's mom.

She smiles before breaking into tears. Her phone dings again. It is a text from Beau.

BEAU (TEXT): Hey Ives, we need to talk.

Ivy takes a deep breath and sighs.

IVY: Shit.

INT. IVY'S BEDROOM - NIGHT

Ivy stares at her daughter and counts as the baby breathes before she finishes her purchase of a one-way ticket. Beau walks in. She closes the laptop.

BOTH: Hey.

INT. IVY'S LIVING ROOM - DAY

Ivy is cooking breakfast as Beau comes down the stairs carrying Caroline. Beau places Caroline in her highchair, before joining Ivy at the stove.

BEAU: I can finish that, you go sit down, Love.

Beau kisses her cheek, and Ivy sits and watches him. Beau shows off his cooking skills, making it into a show for Ivy.

IVY: MasterChef Beau is in the house. Today, he is making pancakes with a special ingredient: bacon. Will he complete it in time before his daughter starts to cry?

Beau flips the pancake successfully.

BEAU: AND HE DOES!

IVY: HE DOES! WOO!

Beau and Ivy dance and laugh loudly around the kitchen with each other.

BEAU: I missed us.

IVY: Yeah, me too.

Ivy and Beau kiss.

BEAU: You and her. This is it for me. There's nothing else. You are my everything.

Beau picks up Caroline.

IVY: She is so beautiful.

BEAU: Little Miss Caroline Jamie Arden, you are the universe and all the stars.

IVY: Do you ever miss her?

BEAU: Every day I go to work, I miss her. She's my baby girl.

IVY: No, do you ever miss Jamie?

> *Beau keeps staring at Caroline, but his eyes are saddened.*

BEAU: *(switching the subject)* Let's eat breakfast. This baby looks hungry, and you wouldn't like her when she's hungry.

IVY: Beau, what happened to you guys? You never told me about it.

BEAU: It doesn't matter. I'm here with you. And Jamie is wherever Jamie is.

IVY: Why are you so mad about it?

BEAU: Ives, Love, please just drop it, okay?

IVY: Okay, sorry. I'll drop it. *(Beat.)* But genuinely, how does that just happen? You were best friends, I mean, you named our daughter after her.

BEAU: I don't know, Ives.

IVY: Crazy.

Ivy starts to eat her breakfast and Beau feeds Caroline.

INT. IVY'S BEDROOM - NIGHT
Ivy and Beau are getting ready for bed together.

BEAU: How's the search for a new guitarist going?

IVY: Well, it's become more like a search for a new band.

BEAU: Oh no. So, what's their new name?

IVY: The Vines, all they did was drop the Ivy.

Beau kisses her forehead.

BEAU: I'm sorry, Ives. Don't worry, you'll find your people, I'm sure. You don't even need a band, you're enough. Imagine it. Next on stage, Ivy Augustine Ellis.

Beau starts mimicking a crowd cheering.

IVY: Yeah, that's the hope.

BEAU: You're already amazing, the world just needs to see you. And even when it does, it's not ready for you. I love you, good night, love.

IVY: Good night, Beau.

EXT. THE PARK - DAY

Ivy and Beau play with Caroline at the park, appearing to be a very happy

*family. Ivy's mom sits on a bench
nearby watching.*

IVY: I need to take a rest, Beau.

BEAU: No worries, Love. I got her.

*Beau kisses her cheek before Ivy goes
and sits with her mom. When Ivy is no
longer watching, Beau pulls a ring box
out of his jacket pocket and shows
Caroline.*

BEAU: Caroline, a week from today, we'll
come back here to this park. Where me and
your mom had our first kiss, and I'm going
to ask her a really important question.
Would that be okay with you, baby girl?

Caroline giggles.

BEAU: I'll take that as a yes.

*Beau hides the ring again as Ivy
returns. He winks at Caroline.*

INT. IVY'S BEDROOM - DAY

Ivy is packing up all of her and Beau's things. She is packing her car and leaving Beau's things outside on the driveway. Caroline is crying in Ivy's mom's arms. Ivy's mom is begging.

IVY'S MOM: Please don't go, please.

IVY: I have to.

IVY'S MOM: No, you don't. What about her?

IVY: Mom, we both know I was never meant to be her mom, please, we talked about this, Beau takes her. And we move on because I can't live a lie. I can't be something I'm not. I'm not her mom; I'll never be her mom. It wouldn't be fair to any of us if I stayed and forced myself into a role not meant for me.

IVY'S MOM: You don't love your own child?

IVY: I love her so much. Why do you think I'm doing this?

Ivy's mom shakes her head.

IVY: I should've never had her in the first place.

IVY'S MOM: You don't mean that.

IVY: I do, though. *(Beat.)* Every time I look at her, I think why did I bring her into this mess? I have nothing to give her. I'm not right. I failed her already just by having her. I know you know, mom. That's how you look at me. I don't want her to ever experience that feeling. It'll be better if I'm nothing but an idea. It's more forgivable than the reality. So as my mother, as the one person who will show me love and forgive me, no matter what I do, please, let me go and let Beau take Caroline.

Ivy's mom looks down at the baby in her arms and back at Ivy.

IVY: Please, mom. It's the only way. It's me or them. You have to pick me.

IVY'S MOM: Ivy, promise me you'll come back.

Ivy hugs her mom before getting in her car and driving away.

PART TWO, CHAPTER FIVE

INT. HOTEL ROOM - MORNING

An older Ivy wakes up in bed with an older Beau beside her.

BEAU: Good morning, love.

IVY: Morning.

Beau puts his glasses on and reads the paper in bed. Ivy gets up and looks out the window at the view of the New York City skyline.

IVY: I'm hungry.

BEAU: Ivy, we can get breakfast once you wake up.

Ivy is confused.

IVY: I am awake.

BEAU: No, you're not. You gotta wake up, Ives. Wake up, Ivy.

IVY: Stop! Beau, stop it! This isn't funny. I'm awake!

BEAU: No, you're not.

IVY: What makes you think I'm not?

BEAU: I'm dead, Ivy.

Beau's face turns pale and there is blood on Ivy's hands.

INT. IVY'S LIVING ROOM - NIGHT
Ivy wakes up alone on her couch.

IVY: Beau!

Audrey, on the other couch, wakes up and they talk.

AUDREY: Was it the same dream again?

IVY: Yeah.

AUDREY: I'll go make us some tea and we'll talk about it.

Audrey goes to the kitchen and Ivy
follows. Ivy sits on the counter.

AUDREY: Do you still love him?

IVY: He was the only person who ever loved
me.

AUDREY: But did you love him? Or did you
just love the way he loved you?

IVY: Why would you ask that?

AUDREY: Because it's very easy to get
confused. Did you love him, or do you just
regret what you did to him?

Ivy stays silent.

AUDREY: You know full well that I'm guiding
you in the right direction. It's hard, but
this is the stuff you have to think about.
I'm your sister. It's my job to teach you
life lessons or whatever.

IVY: Right.

AUDREY: You told me before you feel like you're running but you didn't know what you're running from. Well, have you ever considered that you're running away from yourself because you're too afraid to actually do the difficult part of confronting your faults and all the harm you caused. *(Beat.)* Beau is gone. There is no way to get forgiveness from him. There is no way to fix that with him. There's only you left. You have to do it for yourself.

IVY: I hate how right you are.

AUDREY: It's not me you're mad at, you know that.

IVY: His funeral is tomorrow.

AUDREY: Are you sure you're going to go?

IVY: I have to know. I have to see it for real that he's gone. If I don't, I'll always just keep thinking I can go back to him and I want to meet her. I mean, she's

mine. She's my daughter. She's my baby. And
she lost her dad. She lost Beau.

Ivy tears up and Audrey hugs her.

EXT. CHURCH - DAY

*Ivy stands outside the church doors.
She takes a breath before grabbing the
door handle. She stays frozen until
someone opens the other door, she
steps aside as funeral guests walk
out. Ivy finally steps inside the
church stands staring at the beautiful
funeral set up at the front.*

INT. CHURCH - DAY

*Ivy stays hidden at the back of the
church and watches the video of Beau's
life with Jamie and Caroline.*

INT. CHURCH - DAY

*She slowly walks forward through the
crowd of people leaving until she sees
Caroline and Jamie.*

IVY: *(softly)* Hi, Jamie. Can I talk to you?

JAMIE: Sweet girl, can you go over there?

CAROLINE: Okay, Auntie J.

Caroline goes to help Lily who is cleaning up.

IVY: She's so big now.

JAMIE: What are you doing here?

IVY: *(calmly)* I just wanted to share my condolences.

JAMIE: You don't know what happened, do you?

IVY: Jamie, I just wanted to come pay my respects. Don't make it a bad thing.

JAMIE: You should leave now.

Jamie tries to walk away, Ivy grabs Jamie's arm, stopping her.

IVY: *(desperate)* Let me meet her. Please. I just want to meet her.

JAMIE: You thought the best time to meet her would be during her dad's funeral?

IVY: I know the timing is bad, but I want to meet her. She needs her mom. Now more than ever and that's me. I'm her mom. Please, she's my kid.

JAMIE: She's not your kid. She stopped being yours when you left them. When you abandoned your baby and broke my best friend's heart. When you left him with nothing. And then you came back and took some more. They were fine without you. I had them. I helped him rebuild everything you broke when you left. You left them, never forget that.

IVY: *(full of regret)* I'm sorry, I'm so sorry.

JAMIE: It's too late for that. Beau is dead. Caroline's almost five. You missed every opportunity to be a decent person a long time ago.

Jamie wipes away tears.

JAMIE: He is gone. And she is not yours. No. She is mine. Mine.

Jamie starts to cry. Caroline runs over to comfort her. Caroline gets upset.

CAROLINE: *(to Ivy)* You're mean. Go away. You made Auntie J cry. That's not nice.

Ivy hugs Caroline.

IVY: I'm sorry.

Caroline pushes Ivy away. Ivy keeps holding on as Caroline hits and screams.

CAROLINE: No, no, no. Go away. Go, go, go.

IVY: My sweet girl, I'm sorry.

Ivy starts to cry as she lets Caroline go. Ivy stands there clutching her penny necklace watching as Caroline hugs Jamie.

IVY: I really did love them, Jamie. I really did.

Ivy walks away. Ivy realises this is the last time she will see Caroline. Ivy takes one look back before exiting out the church doors.

INT. IVY'S BEDROOM - LATE AFTERNOON
Ivy and Beau sit beside each other.

BEAU: Ives, I love you, but this... I'm just going to say it. We haven't seen each other in weeks, I know you hate hanging out with me and I think we need to-

IVY: Beau, I'm pregnant.

BEAU: What?

IVY: I'm pregnant.

Beau sits quietly.

IVY: I want to keep it.

BEAU: This is real?

Ivy shows him the tests.

IVY: It's real. I went to the doctor's to confirm it and it's really real and they told me how far along I am. I think it might have happened the night of the dance. I mean that's the only time we didn't have, well you know, you were there. The timeline adds up. I'm sorry. I know it's a shock, but I think this could be amazing. I mean, it's you and me, Beau. We're having a baby.

BEAU: I'm sorry, I need to go... I need Jamie.

Beau leaves. Ivy lies down and lets her tears fall down the side of her face.

Ivy sits in her car and watches as Jamie and Caroline exit the church. She sees Jamie carry Caroline in her arms and fix Caroline's hair before Caroline kisses Jamie's cheek. Jamie and Caroline softly smile at each other. Caroline rests her head on Jamie's shoulder as if it's the softest spot in the universe. There is a sense of calm, there is no nervousness or fear in either of them. Despite the sadness, Jamie and Caroline are perfect.

PART TWO, CHAPTER SIX

Ivy sits in her car, building up the courage to drive away. Lily walks toward the car and knocks on the window. She points to the lock. Ivy lowers the window.

LILY: Hi, can we talk? I'm Lily, I don't know if you know me.

IVY: No, I know you. Beau talked about you. You were friends.

LILY: Yeah, so can we talk?

Ivy unlocks the door and Lily sits down.

LILY: Jamie's been my best friend since I moved to this town. I know that I've never compared to Beau, but she's been my girl, and I will do everything to protect her. And if I'm being honest, if you think Jamie's upset you're here, you have no idea where I'm at. But that's not why I'm in your car, talking to you. I'm here to ask, why? Why are you here? What do you want to do? Do you want to come and take Caroline away? Want to go to court and fight for visitation rights? You won't win. I'm sorry if this is a lot, but have you been thinking of them the last few years or is this new? Because you found out he died? Did you come here with a plan? Or just come to see if my grieving best friend could provide you with some comfort about the death of the love of her life? Did you have some burning questions about Beau, or Caroline, or the life they built without you that needed to be answered? Because if you did, I'm here. You can ask me. I've been here, like a fly on the wall, since the start. Since before you invited that beautiful boy to sit down next to you at that dance. Ivy, I don't think you knew what you started back then, but now it's over. It needs to be over. So, take this time now to get that closure you so badly need to heal whatever you need to heal in order to feel better about all the decisions you made, but don't you dare go near my girls ever again. *(Beat.)* So, what is it that you need to know?

INT. HOSPITAL - DAY

Ivy enters the hospital doors and struggles to walk up to the check in desk.

IVY: Hi, my name is Ivy Augustine Ellis and I'm having a baby and my doctor is Dr. Hunters.

The contractions hit once again and her water breaks. The nurse checks her in, and they rush her to labour and delivery. Ivy gives birth alone with no one to hold her hand. It is an immensely difficult and painful birth. Finally, Caroline is born and placed on Ivy's chest. As Ivy looks at this tiny baby, there is nothing to say, except:

IVY: I'm sorry.

IVY: My sweet girl. I'm sorry.

INT. HOSPITAL - DAY

Ivy sits with her mom and Audrey.

IVY: You should've seen Caroline's face. She was so angry with me. I was nothing but a stranger to her.

Ivy's mom holds her hand.

IVY: I know that's what I expected but actually seeing her. She is so big now, she's not a baby anymore. She jumped in front of Jamie. She's strong, protective, and loving... (*beat.*) She's just like Beau. I mean, she has my hair and at a glance you'd think she's a mini version of me, but that little face, that face that was so angry at me, was Beau's. It felt exactly like he was looking at me with such sad

255

eyes. And there was nothing left to do but leave.

> *Ivy pauses for a long time. Ivy's mom and Audrey look at each other as Ivy takes a breath before speaking again.*

IVY: Jamie was right. I am not her mother.

AUDREY: Do you really believe that?

IVY: It's the truth. Everything Jamie and Lily said. There's no fight. There was never a fight. They were always meant to be with Jamie, I mean, really.

AUDREY: But she's your kid, don't you want to be part of her life?

IVY: I know she's okay and that's enough for me. I can't change the past, but I can let Jamie give her what I could never bring myself to.

IVY'S MOM: I'm proud of how far you've come, Ivy, but do you really think she's better off with Jamie?

IVY: Beau trusted her to be in Caroline's life. There's a reason he held on to her. *(Beat.)* Beau loved Jamie his entire life. She did what I couldn't.

Ivy takes a deep breath.

IVY: She loved him back. *(Beat.)* I trust in that. *I trust in her.*

Ivy holds her mom's hand and kisses it.

EXT. JAMIE'S HOUSE - DAY
Jamie is putting the last boxes in the car. Caroline is sitting in her car seat.

YOUNG ADULT JAMIE: Caroline, how are you feeling?

CAROLINE: I feel sad.

YOUNG ADULT JAMIE: Is it because we're leaving?

CAROLINE: Yeah.

YOUNG ADULT JAMIE: That's okay. You're allowed to be sad. It is sad. I'm sad too.

CAROLINE: You're sad too?

YOUNG ADULT JAMIE: Yeah. *(Beat.)* Thank you for sharing your feelings with me.

CAROLINE: It's okay to be sad. And it's good to talk about it.

YOUNG ADULT JAMIE: Remember that you never have to be sad by yourself. *(Beat.)* Okay, you listen carefully, Caroline.

CAROLINE: I'm listening, Auntie J.

Caroline giggles.

YOUNG ADULT JAMIE: I'm here. I will always be here. You can always talk to me. About anything you want.

> *Jamie goes and sits in the driver's seat.*

CAROLINE: Anything?

YOUNG ADULT JAMIE: Yes. Anything, baby girl.

> *Jamie looks at Caroline in the rearview mirror.*

CAROLINE: Do you think daddy's still alive in other universes?

YOUNG ADULT JAMIE: I think so. That's something nice to think about.

CAROLINE: I miss him.

YOUNG ADULT JAMIE: I do too. (Beat.) Are you ready to go?

Caroline nods and hugs Beau's teddy
bear. Jamie takes a breath before
driving away. A file folder with
Caroline's name on it and a brochure
titled "Project Invisible Best
Friend". is seen peeking out of
Jamie's bag.

PART THREE:
MY I.NVISIBLE B.EST F.RIEND

(THE PLAY THAT STARTED IT ALL)

PART THREE, CHAPTER ONE

INT. CAROLINE'S BEDROOM - NIGHT
CAROLINE, a 15-year-old girl and FLYNN, her best friend, are sitting next to each other on the floor talking to each other.

FLYNN: So, you seriously would choose to eat a pickle wrapped in raw bacon with a side of mayonnaise than run naked wearing Christmas antlers through Times Square?

CAROLINE: Well yeah, at least I could do it without anyone seeing me.

FLYNN: I'd be there.

CAROLINE: Well, whatever. Have fun watching that.

FLYNN: I'll make sure to bring a bucket.

CAROLINE: Okay, your turn.

FLYNN: Okay, just don't ask me anything too scary or gross.

CAROLINE: Oh, and mayonnaise and raw bacon isn't gross, goodness, don't be a girl.

FLYNN: Excuse me, that's offensive to yourself, you are, in fact, a girl.

CAROLINE: *(in a mocking tone)* That's offensive.

> *Flynn and Caroline mock each other, gradually growing less articulate, losing clarity as they speak.*

FLYNN: Enough. What was your question?

CAROLINE: Okay, here it is. If you had to choose five people to have at your dinner table, anyone past or present, fictional or real, who'd sit at your table?

> *Flynn freezes up, the question causes him distress.*

FLYNN: That's a really tough question, C. Just give me a second.

CAROLINE: I got all the time in the world.

FLYNN: Okay, so I'd have Elvis, Cleopatra, Teddy Roosevelt, and the dude who invented silly string. I'd love to know what was going on in his head when that happened.

CAROLINE: That's only four. I said five.

FLYNN: *(struggling to answer)* You... need to be patient. I need a little more time to think of a fifth person. I think that's gotta be the most important seat, so I gotta make sure I give it to someone really, really important. Don't you think?

> *Caroline goes to ask more about it but is interrupted by a knock on her door. Aunt Jamie walks in.*

AUNT JAMIE: Alright, bedtime. Get those teeth brushed and get some sleep.

CAROLINE: Yeah yeah, I know

> *Caroline rolls her eyes and makes a goofy face at Flynn following her. Aunt Jamie stops her before the door.*

AUNT JAMIE: How was today? Those headaches still bothering you?

CAROLINE: *(lying)* Not too bad today.

Caroline and Flynn attempt to move past but fail.

AUNT JAMIE: Okay, well, kid, remember to tell me if they start up again, and don't forget to take your meds before sleep.

Aunt Jamie moves out of the way of the door.

AUNT JAMIE: *(playfully)* Goodnight, with love.

Caroline jokingly curtsies.

CAROLINE: *(playfully)* With love.

Caroline and Aunt Jamie hug before Caroline finally gets out the door, Flynn follows her. Aunt Jamie sits on Caroline's bed looking frustrated and

AUNT JAMIE: Beau, I promise you, I'll find
a way to stop it. I promise.

*Aunt Jamie hugs the picture frame for
just a moment before putting it back
as Caroline and Flynn enter the room
again.*

CAROLINE: I know you love me but it's time
to get out of my room.

AUNT JAMIE: Are you sure you don't want to
have a cuddle party with your favourite
auntie?

*Tickle fight ensues between Caroline
and Auntie, Flynn laughs watching from
the side.*

CAROLINE: No, no, I'm too old, stop stop
stop!

AUNT JAMIE: You will always be Beau's baby girl to me. Now I will leave the room, but don't stay up being dumb.

CAROLINE: Too late, already dumb.

AUNT JAMIE: I love you.

CAROLINE: In this universe?

AUNT JAMIE: In any and all universes!

CAROLINE: I love you too, Auntie J

Aunt Jamie leaves.

INT. DOCTOR'S OFFICE - DAY
> *The Doctor is talking on the phone while pacing around the office.*

DOCTOR: *(on the phone)* I know, we predicted the shutdown to be a few months ago. Trust me, the Caroline Arden case is my top priority. She is rare and the last hope of this project. Look, I know you're upset with me for the last screw up, but in my

defence, the others… Yes, I know. I know. I
KNOW, do not shut me down, please I
promise. I can prove that Project I.B.F
works, and if not, you can do what you will
with me.

INT. CAROLINE'S ROOM - DAY
*Caroline and Flynn are sitting across
from each other. Caroline is painting.*

CAROLINE: Do you love me?

FLYNN: Of course, why wouldn't I? You're my
best friend.

CAROLINE: No, like... really, really love
me?

FLYNN: You know it's impossible for me to
know right?

CAROLINE: Nothing's impossible. (*Beat.*) And
shouldn't you know your own feelings?

FLYNN: It's not that simple, C.

CAROLINE: What is complicated about this? I know how I feel. Why don't you?

FLYNN: How can I know my love is real?

CAROLINE: You sound just like my doctor. She's always talking, making me think about questions like that. She makes me question a lot of things. Sometimes it hurts my head.

FLYNN: Maybe, you... need to stop asking so many questions and finish your painting.

CAROLINE: Okay, whatever, you say, kind sir.

FLYNN: What are you even painting? Is that a dog?

> *Caroline looks at Flynn with annoyance. Flynn picks up the painting trying to figure it out.*

CAROLINE: You're so mean, God. It's supposed to be you.

FLYNN: Okay, so I'm mean and being compared to a dog now. What is this?

CAROLINE: Shut up, you're dumb.

FLYNN: Whatever, you meanie.

CAROLINE: I am actually offended by that statement.

FLYNN: I am actually offended by your face.

CAROLINE: Now you've crossed the line of offensive.

FLYNN: Have I now?

CAROLINE: Yes, now you really owe me. Answer my question about the dinner party.

FLYNN: *(hesitant)* You... need to stop... I'll tell you when I have an answer. And right now, I don't. *(To himself.)* No... Not yet.

INT. DOCTOR'S OFFICE - DAY

The Doctor is looking over Caroline's files. The Doctor is clearly upset. Caroline walks in with Aunt Jamie and a nurse. Caroline sits in a chair across from the Doctor who starts to write notes. Nurse and Aunt Jamie leave.

DOCTOR: So, Caroline, how has your day been going so far?

CAROLINE: Well, today I played Monopoly with Flynn and completely obliterated him across the board. Umm... I finished my painting. It's Flynn. See? He thought it was a dog! What an idiot. It's clearly him, right? You see, it's totally Flynn. Caroline holds up scribbles on a white paper.

DOCTOR: Flynn is really your friend, isn't he?

CAROLINE: Of course, he's my best friend. He's my only friend.

DOCTOR: Caroline, can you tell me about him, again?

CAROLINE: Flynn's a complete dork. He's so funny, like "shoot milk out of your nose" funny. He gives really good hugs and is really patient with me. He listens to me. *(Beat.)* He has the most intense knowledge of random trivia. Like he once explained to me in full detail how starfish grow back their limbs. And...

DOCTOR: When did he first appear in your life, can you please tell me about that, Caroline?

CAROLINE: I first met him when I was seven.

DOCTOR: That was eight years ago, correct?

CAROLINE: Yes.

DOCTOR: How did you meet him?

CAROLINE: He just showed up one day and introduced himself and ever since then, he has never left my side.

DOCTOR: Caroline, what else can you tell me about that day?

CAROLINE: I don't know what to say, I just woke up and he was there.

DOCTOR: Where did you wake up? What did the room look like?

CAROLINE: I was in my room; I just woke up from my nap.

DOCTOR: Caroline, where were you actually?

CAROLINE: Okay, it wasn't my room. It was... the playroom and I was playing with my dolls. Flynn tapped me on my shoulder and-

DOCTOR: Caroline, please... Seriously now, what room was it?

CAROLINE: *(with difficulty.)* Fine. *(Beat.)* It was… it was… cold. There were a lot of lights everywhere. It's hard to remember.

DOCTOR: You are doing perfectly. Please continue. Tell me, who was in the room with you?

CAROLINE: Flynn was there when I opened my eyes.

DOCTOR: Do you remember who was in the room when you went to sleep?

CAROLINE: There was a nurse, a couple of nurses, Auntie J was there. And you. I remember now, you were there too. Why were you all in my room?

Caroline starts to panic.

DOCTOR: Because it wasn't your room, Caroline. I need you to listen to me very carefully right now. Ten years ago, you were selected as part of a mission. An important mission. Caroline... Please listen... You asked him something... You asked him a question about a dinner party... Please, Caroline...

CAROLINE: No, you're lying. We do this every time, just stop it.

Caroline stands. Aunt Jamie stops her from leaving.

DOCTOR: You are aware that it is highly unusual for you to still have your imaginary friend. I am just trying to help you.

CAROLINE: Flynn is not imaginary.

AUNT JAMIE: Caroline...

CAROLINE: He's real. I can feel him. I can hold him. He can hold me. We spend all day together and he stays by my side through everything. He is real. I know he is. He is the only person in this life that has been here for me. Who was holding my hand through storms when thunder would scare me? Or who was the one who held me when I'd

cry? All because of the side effects of
those stupid pills you make me take. It was
never you. Not the doctor. I grew up in
that room all alone. I don't even get to go
to school like a normal kid. It's just the
house and the doctor's office. I know
nothing anymore except this, that room, and
him. I don't want to remember what my life
was before you took me away. I don't want
anything or anyone else. Only Flynn. And
you want to tell me he isn't real? Don't
give me something actually good, just to
take it away. I don't want to lose him too.

*Caroline begins to scream and sob and
starts breaking down.*

CAROLINE: Don't you dare. No, no, no, don't
you dare take him away. He's all I have.

*The doctor and nurse come in. Auntie
holds Caroline. They sedate her and
she begins to fall asleep. Flynn comes
in and gets her up off the ground.
Flynn carries her unconscious body out
of the office. As Flynn walks out the*

INT. CAROLINE'S ROOM - DAY
*Flynn lays her on her bed and sits
next to her.*

FLYNN: *(to himself.)* C, I told you so many times, they aren't ever going to believe you. I'm not real. I'm just here for you. All I know is you. I just woke up one day and you were there. "Hello, my name is Flynn and I'm your best friend," I remember meeting you for the first time, how you didn't say a word. You stayed away. You didn't even notice me there, but I didn't mind at all because it was you. My Caroline. I knew you before you knew me. I knew all your favourite things without you saying... You love the colour purple because it reminds you of the Jello they gave you when they brought you here. And your favourite animal is a giraffe because you couldn't believe such a weird creature could exist. I knew about that even before those rants you gave about their unnecessarily long necks. I knew from the very moment I woke up, I had to stay by your side. You were just so innocent but so sad. You didn't deserve that pain. That loss. And I knew that...

I knew I needed to protect you from all harm but now I have lied to you so many times. I'm failing you. I've spent so many nights trying to come up with any valid excuse for what I've done. I've promised a forever I can't give... because one day you'll know the truth, and you'll finally lose me to reality. I've known what I am for a very long time... It was wrong of me to keep that from you. I hate that I kept it from you. (Beat.) I just wanted to stay a little bit longer, but you deserve the world.

And... I can give that to you. I just want to make you happy, and you say I do, but I know I can't forever. I was never meant to. Letting you go is going to be the hardest thing for me to do but it's for you, so... It will be okay.

Maybe if I never existed, you would've been okay, maybe even better that way. But this process, it's not that simple. I'm trying to make it easier but there are instructions and programs, and everything was set from the beginning. I need to let you go now. I know the words you have to say, words you have said, and the words I was supposed to say.
Those words. They will be my last gift to you, my best friend. I have to leave you soon and I'm sorry. I'm so very sorry *(beat.)* because once I go away, I can't come back, so this is my goodbye.

Flynn stays watching Caroline with sad eyes for a long while before kissing her forehead, waking her up.

CAROLINE: *(softly.)* Flynn...

FLYNN: Hey... so are you going to tell me what happened back there?

CAROLINE: Do we have to do this? I know you know already... You don't need to pretend like you don't.

FLYNN: You didn't need to get us locked up in this room again.

CAROLINE: I'm sorry, but they just kept saying that you weren't real.

FLYNN: They are right though, you know this C, why does it still bother you?

Caroline is silent.

FLYNN: We've talked about this.

CAROLINE: You're real to me, so doesn't that make you real, can't that be enough?

There is a pause as Flynn contemplates Caroline's question.

FLYNN: I don't know.

CAROLINE: I do. I know.

FLYNN: But you have to stop telling them that. I'm not real to them like I am to you. It'll only get you into trouble.

CAROLINE: I don't care how many times she locks us in here. *(Beat.)* As long as we're together... nothing else is important.

FLYNN: Still, C, there is an entire world out-

CAROLINE: I like being alone with you. Don't you like being with me?

FLYNN: Of course, C, but…

CAROLINE: But what?

FLYNN: Aren't you curious?

CAROLINE: Curious?

FLYNN: About the world? What's beyond these walls?

CAROLINE: No, I've already got my entire world right in front of me.

FLYNN: But don't you want to know what it's like to breathe fresh air? To live a normal life? Go to school? Don't you want to know more than just this house.

CAROLINE: Do you want to leave? Is that what you're trying to tell me? Are you getting sick of me?

FLYNN: That's not what I'm saying. I'm saying you deserve more than just this. *(Beat.)* More than me. You deserve the world. You deserve to see it and be in it. I know you're dying to know. I know your dreams, C. All of them. And you're never going to be able to do any of it if you're locked up in this place. I don't want to hold you back.

CAROLINE: Don't blame yourself. They're the ones who refuse to accept the truth.

FLYNN: What if one day you do find out the truth? Would you be happy?

CAROLINE: All I know is that it would be nice to know what's real and what's not.

FLYNN: What happens if you find out for a fact that I'm not?

CAROLINE: Not what? Not real?

FLYNN: Yeah, exactly, I'm not real enough, C.

CAROLINE: Don't say that. No. No. Don't.

FLYNN: Hey, hey, I'm sorry... It's okay.

CAROLINE: Don't you dare say those words again. You're real. I... I know you are. You are real. I'm not crazy. You're real. I'm not crazy. You're real. I'm not crazy. I'm not crazy. I'm not crazy. You are real.

Flynn holds her in his arms as she has another panic attack repeating those words.

288

PART THREE, CHAPTER TWO

INT. DOCTOR'S OFFICE - DAY
The Doctor and Aunt Jamie talk about Caroline.

DOCTOR: She is still in denial.

AUNT JAMIE: She still truly believes, even after all these years. With what happened to the others that Lily told us about, how has she survived this long with him still there?

DOCTOR: She knows that he isn't real right?

AUNT JAMIE: I don't know, she must, but she always says these things.

Aunt Jamie plays a recording on her phone.

CAROLINE: I believe, don't you - don't you believe he's real. He's real to me, so that makes him real. Stop, stop, STOP. I know you're recording so stop it. He is real because I see him, and I feel him. That makes him real. He's real.

AUNT JAMIE: So, she might be aware that he isn't real but chooses to believe anyway.

DOCTOR: Maybe that's what's keeping her alive.

AUNT JAMIE: Her belief is what's keeping her alive?

DOCTOR: Yes, she's the only one left. Don't you remember the others, they were so close to being done when…

AUNT JAMIE: Doctor, I'm sorry but that's too insane of a theory. Belief is what makes her different?

DOCTOR: Artificial friends implanted into children's brains is insane, but you were there when we did that, you were there when this began, so why are you just now thinking like this?

AUNT JAMIE: I thought this was going to end differently. We were only supposed to help, not this. You said you didn't want any more kids losing their imaginations or growing up alone and in pain. You said it would let them stay kids a little longer. Caroline, with what she went through... Finding her dad on the bathroom floor… I can't even imagine... He was all she had, her mother was gone, and he tried to stay for her, he did... but he just couldn't... *(beat.)* He was my best friend. I cannot fail her like I failed him. I thought I was doing the right thing, bringing her into this. I begged you to let her in, despite the conflict of interest. Despite Lily warning me of the endless risks. But you made me believe she'd be safer here. This project was made for people like them. It was meant to save them from themselves. With everything that was happening. People were dying from loneliness. This was supposed to protect her... them, but now... The glitch... They were supposed to be happy. This wasn't how it was supposed to go.

DOCTOR: You were in charge of keeping her and the others stable through this whole process, if anything you are to blame for all t-

AUNT JAMIE: You're blaming this on me? *Project IBF* was your vision, your invention, your life. You're the one who put the damn thing in their heads and couldn't get them out. You are lucky enough to even have me here. How many people have we lost? How many children? How many did we lose? Tell me, doctor, how many?

> *Aunt Jamie says "doctor" in a cynical tone, questioning whether she deserves the title. The doctor looks at Aunt Jamie with a look of sadness and hopelessness as she wishes she could have a different answer.*

> *The two sit in silence as if giving all those lost a moment of grief.*

PART THREE, CHAPTER THREE

INT. CAROLINE'S ROOM - DAY

Nurse gives Caroline medicine and then leaves. Caroline spits out the pills before joining Flynn. Flynn and Caroline sit on the bed playing a game where they mirror each other.

CAROLINE: Ever think about the fact mirrors could just be portals to other dimensions, but your "reflection" is always blocking the way?

FLYNN: Exactly how many drugs do they give you in this place?

CAROLINE: Shut up.

Flynn laughs at her, and Caroline looks slightly annoyed then smiles.

CAROLINE: Dude, seriously, what if the Multiverse theory is right and there are an infinite number of other realities. Infinite different versions of us, of this room, of the world. What if there's a universe where pigs can actually fly, or

trees are purple or even one where ice
cream is hot? Like, imagine we somehow
travel to another, different version of
this place and it's nice. And we weren't
stuck in this room, in this hospital
forever. And I could visit the forest and
pet a frog.

FLYNN: Why a frog? Aren't they covered in
slime or something? And since when do you
care about the outside world? I thought you
had your entire world right in front of
you. Am I not enough for you now?

CAROLINE: As much as I hate to admit it,
you got to me, okay? I do want more and,
sure, frogs are slimy but that's not the
point. What if there's a universe out there
where we're free? What if there's a reality
where I was never brought to this... this
place? What if there's a universe where I
have parents, a house, a backyard, a white
fence, and a dog named Pickle who knows how
to catch frisbees in his mouth? (*Beat.*) Of
course, we're neighbours. Yeah, you live on
one side of us, and Auntie J lives on the

other, because of course, you can't separate her and dad. And we have a treehouse together and we hang out basically every day, except on family movie night when my mom insists on "family time." But every other night we hang out and play games and paint and do all the things we do every day in this universe.

FLYNN: Why would I be there? You'd have your family. You wouldn't need me. I wouldn't be a thing...

> *Caroline covers her ears and sings loud enough not to hear him.*

FLYNN: *(grabs her hands and holds them.)* I get it, I'll stop, calm down.

> *Flynn takes her hands and makes her get up off the bed. They begin to dance slowly as Flynn hums her lullaby to calm Caroline down before the conversation continues.*

CAROLINE: Also, the "parallel universe you" isn't an annoying killjoy.

FLYNN: *(Dramatically.)* Oh, I can't bear to live with such an insult, oh my heart.

CAROLINE: And parallel Flynn actually tells me who the fifth person at his table is.

FLYNN: *(struggling.)* You... You're still stuck on that.

CAROLINE: Yes, very much stuck. I need to know who's fifth at your table.

FLYNN: You... Do you really?

CAROLINE: Yes, if it's the last thing I do, I will get that answer out of you.

FLYNN: I doubt it's that important.

CAROLINE: It really is. *(Begs.)* Please tell me, please, please tell me whose butt takes up chair number five.

    Flynn is silent.

CAROLINE: You know how I hate not knowing things, why must you torture me like this?

FLYNN: Because it's my job. I am your best friend, aren't I?

CAROLINE: No, I hate you.

FLYNN: Okay.

CAROLINE: Excuse me, I just said that I hate you.

FLYNN: And I said okay.

CAROLINE: You're supposed to react. Why are you like this?

FLYNN: Because if I was any different, you'd actually hate me.

CAROLINE: Shut up.

FLYNN: I bet there's another you for every universe, and if I could, I'd search every

one of those infinite realities in hopes of
meeting every version of you.

>   *She looks at him and smiles.*

CAROLINE: Aw.

FLYNN: You wanna know why?

CAROLINE: Yes, of course, I do.

FLYNN: Because in the infinite amount of
yous there'd be, I bet I could find at
least one... *(Beat.)* That's less annoying
than the real you.

CAROLINE: *(Offended.)* Hey...

FLYNN: I was just joking, I promise.

>   *Flynn and Caroline sit in silence for
>   a moment before Caroline breaks it and
>   moves closer to Flynn.*

CAROLINE: Why do you stay with me if you
think I'm so annoying?

Flynn stays silent.

CAROLINE: Do you want to?

FLYNN: Want to what?

CAROLINE: Leave.

FLYNN: Even if I did, I couldn't.

CAROLINE: Why?

FLYNN: I don't know.

CAROLINE: Are you sure?

FLYNN: Yes, and even if I did know, I wouldn't want to leave you.

INT. DOCTOR'S OFFICE - DAY

DOCTOR: You know I didn't see any of this, I didn't think any of this would happen.

INT. CAROLINE'S ROOM - DAY

CAROLINE: Because you love me.

FLYNN: Even if I do, you know it's not real.

DOCTOR (V.O): I programmed them to only be their best friends.

CAROLINE: I don't care.

FLYNN:(hesitant.) Okay then.

DOCTOR (V.O): I didn't think that they were going to be able to even know what it was, let alone feel it.

CAROLINE: Say it then, if you love me, answer the question.

INT. DOCTOR'S OFFICE - DAY
DOCTOR: I didn't want it to end like this. I don't want to lose her too.

INT. CAROLINE'S ROOM - DAY
  Flynn whispers the answer in
  Caroline's ear. They look at each

other as Caroline processes what he said. They move towards each other as if to kiss. Silently, Caroline falls to the ground. Flynn leans over her. Caroline smiles weakly. She is dying.

INT. DOCTOR'S OFFICE – DAY

DOCTOR: I didn't know they would fall in love.

Aunt Jamie is crying and shaking her head. The Doctor tries to comfort her, but Aunt Jamie runs out the door.

INT. CAROLINE'S ROOM – DAY
Flynn is holding Caroline as she lays on the floor.

FLYNN: *(terrified.)* I'm sorry I didn't say it until now. When you asked that stupid chair question, I knew it was time. My time. But I just couldn't leave. So, I fought against it. I lied. I-I'm sorry. I was supposed to go. No. This isn't what was supposed to happen. I was supposed to be

the one. Only me. You were supposed to see
the world. I was trying to free you.

CAROLINE: *(weakly.)* Hey, don't worry, you'll
find me in another universe, remember?

FLYNN: *(desperate.)* I love you.

> *Caroline's eyes close as she drifts
> into eternal slumber. Flynn kisses her
> forehead. The lights flicker.*

INT. JAMIE'S LIVING ROOM - DAY
> *Aunt Jamie rushes into her house and
> runs straight to Caroline's room. She
> knocks to no response.*

AUNT JAMIE: Caroline, I'm home. *(Beat.)*
Caroline?

> *Aunt Jamie opens the door.*

INT. CAROLINE'S ROOM - DAY
> *Caroline lying alone on the floor.
> Aunt Jamie comes in and finds her*

*body. Aunt Jamie cradles her in her
arms while sobbing violently.*

INT. DOCTOR'S OFFICE - DAY

*The Doctor sits with their head down
as a notification on their computer
announces.*

COMPUTER: Patient C143's Flynn is now
offline. The shutdown phrase "You would be
the fifth person at my table." was used.
Patient C143's Flynn shutdown time was 2311
on 12/17/36.

INT. CAROLINE'S NURSERY - NIGHT

*Beau sits in a rocking chair cradling
Baby Caroline singing her lullaby.*

BEAU: Can I hold you in my arms
Keep you safe and warm
You're the only one I've got
With me anymore

I wanted you to know
You're the reason I stayed here
I don't know what I'd do

Without you, my dear

Just stay with me
And I'll hold you tight
Just stay with me
While the stars dance outside

Hold my hand in yours
Promise to hold on
Close those pretty eyes
Sleep, my Caroline

Just stay with me
And I'll hold you tight
Just stay with me
While the stars dance outside

Just stay with me
Even one more night
Please stay with me
Don't wanna say goodnight
To you, Caroline

*Beau kisses her forehead and the baby
smiles in her sleep.*

BEAU: I love you, my baby. To the moon and
back. In every known and unknown universe.
(Beat.) My girl. My love. My Caroline.

The End.